Josie Bloom

AND THE

EMERGENCY

OF LIFE

Josie Bloom
AND THE
EMERGENCY
OF LIFE

Susan Hill Long

A Paula Wiseman Book

New York   London   Toronto   Sydney   New Delhi

SIMON & SCHUSTER BOOKS FOR YOUNG READERS

An imprint of Simon & Schuster Children's Publishing Division

1230 Avenue of the Americas, New York, New York 10020

SIMON & SCHUSTER BOOKS FOR YOUNG READERS

is a trademark of Simon & Schuster, Inc.

For information about special discounts for bulk purchases, please contact Simon & Schuster Special Sales at 1-866-506-1949 or business@simonandschuster.com.

The Simon & Schuster Speakers Bureau can bring authors to your live event. For more information or to book an event, contact the Simon & Schuster Speakers Bureau at 1-866-248-3049 or visit our website at www.simonspeakers.com.

Book design by Tom Daly

The text for this book was set in Excelsior LT Std.

Manufactured in the United States of America

1119 FFG

First Edition

10 9 8 7 6 5 4 3 2 1

Library of Congress Cataloging-in-Publication Data

Names: Long, Susan Hill, 1965– author.

Title: Josie Bloom and the emergency of life / Susan Long.

Description: First edition. | New York : Simon & Schuster, [2020] | "A Paula Wiseman Book." | Summary: In 1977, middle-schooler Josie secretly takes on her aging grandfather's financial problems while also helping her friend Winky bail his Major League Baseball idol out of the town jail.

Identifiers: LCCN 2019016015|

ISBN 9781534444270 (hardcover) | ISBN 9781534444294 (eBook)

Subjects: | CYAC: Finance, Personal—Fiction. | Grandfathers—Fiction. | Friendship—Fiction. | Baseball—Fiction. | Family life—Maine—Fiction. | Maine—History—20th century—Fiction.

Classification: LCC PZ7.H55742 Jos 2020 | DDC [Fic]—dc23

LC record available at https://lccn.loc.gov/2019016015

This book is dedicated to Alice B. Hill,
with love, admiration, and thanks

The Money

If Grandpa was the one telling this story, he'd probably start with one of his mottoes, such as *Home Is Where You Hang Your Hat*. My best friend, Winky, would roll it out like Joe Viola's evil changeup, a pitch that starts out a fastball, and—surprise!—drops low and slow. Mr. Mee and Mrs. B-B both would probably quote from some book: *There is nothing so strong or safe in an emergency of life as the simple truth.*—Charles Dickens. But I'm the one telling the story, and I say it began with the bologna.

The first time it happened, I was sitting on the couch sorting socks. I patted around the pillows and throws for a missing mate. No luck. I got up and shook out the House of Harmony Church Ladies' Auxiliary Bicentennial Blanket, and out flew a package of bologna. The strange part was, instead of a stack of delicious lunch meat, the package was stuffed with money.

I beelined to the kitchen with my findings. Grandpa was peeling potatoes, the Maine state vegetable. "Why, Josie Bloom," he said. Grandpa scratched his bald spot with the tip of the peeler. "What'd you do, rob a bank?"

"No." I thought about it. "Did you?"

"No-oo-oo," he said, very fishy, like he'd just yanked off the ski mask after pulling the heist.

While he tried to cram the money into his wallet, I asked him a few more questions.

"Did you get an odd job?" Like the time he turned Mrs. Bean's old chipped bathtub into a shrine for the Virgin Mary. "Did you get money from a long-lost relative?" That sort of thing happens, but we don't know of any relatives. "Do you think a burglar might break into the house and rob us?" Because why did he hide it? "You could put it under your mattress." I'd heard people on TV talk about doing that.

Grandpa was not giving me any answers. He seemed out of sorts in a way that if I had that kind of money, I would not be. If I had that kind of money, I'd buy up the entire collection of *Ripley's Believe It or Not!* books. I would probably still have a lot of cash left over, and with the rest I would take a trip to the *Ripley's Believe It or Not!* museum in Orlando, Florida.

"Can I have three dollars?" I said.

Grandpa had managed to shove some of the cash in each of his pockets, and was peeling another potato into the sink, fast as lightning. "It is better to remain silent and be thought a fool," Grandpa said, "than to speak and remove all doubt."

These are words I know all too well. He used a woodworking tool to burn them forever onto a plaque. This was during craft-time at Pineland Senior and Assisted Living over in Topsham, where he used to live with Grandma Kaye until she died of old age, and before he came to live with me.

I'll stop right there and point out that Grandpa came to live with me when my mom died, as he's my only living relative and there was never any dad in the picture. By that I mean, there's a family picture on the shelf in the den, and it's just Mom and me. Whenever I would ask about my dad, she'd tell me he was dead, more or less. "He's dead to me," she'd say. "End of story." Anyway, Mom "expired" of sudden cardiac arrest, which is a problem with the heart's electrical system, and not anybody's fault at all. Even the *Hamburg Catch-up!* reported how Josephine Violet Bloom, age nine, called 911 immediately. When we talked about it, back then, Grandpa took me by the shoulders and looked me in the eye and said, "Josie, there is nothing you could have done, and there is no way to place a call any faster than immediately." But sometimes I wonder. These days, Grandpa would be more apt to snap a salute and say, "Pancakes!"

Anyhow, that plaque (plus other ones) was always trying to get my attention from its shelf in the den. But if you think about it, isn't the fool the one who hides seventy-eight dollars in a package of bologna?

The second time it happened, I was taking out the garbage. I found a wad of rubber-banded bills between the liner and the can under the sink.

"I almost threw it out!" I mentioned.

Grandpa grabbed the bills from my hand and shot a suspicious look at me, the sink, and the garbage can. Then he stomped out of the kitchen.

"Now that money stinks like fish wrapping!" I said to his cardiganed back. "And it's *moist!*"

"Lima beans!" Grandpa blurted from the den.

It was sort of a new thing, a troubling thing, the blurting.

The third time it happened (rolled up in a toilet paper tube!), I didn't tell Grandpa. I put the money in a Keds box under my bed in case I needed it, and soon enough I did.

It gets cold here in Hamburg, Maine. That January, it got wicked cold. There was frost inside the window-panes. Even in my bed, under my covers, with a hot water bottle, it was cold. Turns out Grandpa had not paid the oil bill, and the tank was empty.

"I'll take care of it," said Grandpa. But he didn't. And that's when the water pipes froze—"I'm on it," said Grandpa—and burst. "Don't you worry about a thing," said Grandpa, followed by no running water for two weeks.

I don't remember why I opened up the desk Grandpa calls a secretary, but that's where I found the envelopes. Most of them were stamped in red by somebody with a heavy hand and a bad temper: PAST DUE, or SECOND ATTEMPT, or FINAL NOTICE. I grouped all the envelopes by type and showed them to Grandpa.

"Schlitz!" he blurted. (The name of his favorite beer!)

So. That's how when I started finding the money and Grandpa was blurting about beer quite regular, I had the good idea to take the money I kept finding here and there around the house and put it in the mail-in envelopes that came with the angry notices and which Grandpa was stuffing inside the secretary desk and then blurting about. After that the house was nice and warm, and the water kept on running in the taps. And all because of me! I did it! I felt glad and proud. Grandpa was happy, and he never seemed to notice when the money he hid went missing. I kept secret what I'd done with the money and he quit blurting about Schlitz.

Everything was fine till there came a bill too big to pay.

What's a Mort-gage?

A mortgage," said my best friend, Winky Wheaton. He said it *more-gidge*. "It's what the bank gives people so they can have a house." He fit most of a maple-bar into his mouth. It was a Tuesday morning in March, and we were at school enjoying the free-and-reduced breakfast.

Mrs. Crosier assigned me to Winky on the first day of school back in second grade because he was the new kid. "Winky" seems like a friendly nickname for his given name of Elwyn, except that Winky is legally blind. Stargardt disease. Juvenile macular degeneration. Winky says a nickname makes a person feel accepted, and I say that's like going "Thanks very much!" to the pigeon who poops on your head. I know because of how Becky Schenck calls me "Brillo" on account of my hair, which, I'm sorry to say, is rusty-looking and wiry like an old Brillo pad.

"If it's something the bank gives you," I said to Winky, "then why do they want so much of it back?"

"How it works is, the bank gives you a lot of money, and then you have to pay it all back, plus extra, and *until* you pay it all back, the bank owns the house. My dad spits and moans about it every month."

"Every month!" *What?* "You have to pay it every month?"

"Yup."

Schlitz! Not only did I *not* have one hundred and three dollars and eighty-seven cents to pay the bill *on or before March 15, 1977*, I would need one hundred and three dollars and eighty-seven cents all over again in April! Waiting to maybe find mystery-money in the washing machine or the hamper was obviously not going to be workable, long-term.

I said, "It doesn't seem like a very friendly system."

Winky Wheaton shrugged. Then he leaned over to poke around in his backpack, and he pulled out a book cozy made of quilted fabric—mostly jungle-type flowers and here and there a monkey-head. Winky's mother sews Brenda's Book Cozies straight from a wheelie-cart that slides over her bed, and I had ordered one to cover up the third-quarter health textbook. *Let's Study: Your Body and You*. Rhymes with *euw*.

"I didn't tell Grandpa about the mortgage," I said as I fit the cozy over my book.

Winky wanted to know why not. I could tell because when he's thinking, Winky's eyes turn the gray-green color of Pickerel Pond on a cold day in fall. His hair sticks up and coils all over the place like a bunch of question marks and exclamation points.

"Do you know how hard it is to talk to a serial blurter?" I said to Winky's hair. "I ask him about the money and he salutes and blurts and leaves the room! Grandpa doesn't open those envelopes, and I do."

Winky popped the last bite of his maple-bar into his mouth. "That'sh like a third-baysh coach calling the play at firsht baysh," he said, around the donut.

"Huh?"

He swallowed. "It's not your place."

"Well, if *I* don't take care of it, who will?" I said.

Notice that we'd been talking for all of about

three and a half minutes, and Winky had already
wormed baseball into the conversation. Winky
loves baseball—he loves the sound of the bat and
the ball, the umpire's cry, *stee-rike!*—which is why
I only had to wait about two seconds . . .

"Viola's in a"—Winky lowered his voice and
spelled it out—"S-L-U-M-P."

Winky's Hero

Joe Viola is Winky's all-time favorite baseball player. When the Boston Believers went to the top of the bracket and all the way to the quarterfinals in the '74 World Series? Joe Viola's pitching was all and I mean *all* Winky could talk about. 1974 was very boring in terms of conversation with Winky. If I had a dime for every time I heard that Number 23 has a heart of gold and the soul of a saint and can throw a changeup like the devil himself, well, then I could have all the heating oil and hot water my cold little toes desired.

I said, "A slum—"

"Tssssssssst!" Winky hissed, flapping his hands in my face, "don't say it out loud!"

"All right already!"

"It's bad luck."

"I got it!"

"The Believers will never make it to the playoffs if he doesn't snap out of it. *Last* year during
spring training he was throwing smoke and *slurve
clinch brutal-schedule heat Florida batting mathe-
matically-alive* . . ."

I wasn't really listening at that point. I promise I didn't mean to yawn, but baseball is wicked
dull. The players stand around, they scratch them-
selves, they spit. It's gross.

Let me explain that the whole town of
Hamburg, Maine, is crazy for baseball. Hamburg is
the home of the Hot Dogs, the farm team for the
great Boston Believers. The Hot Dogs play down at
Hot Dogs Field all summer long, and "goin'-the-
game" is what everybody in town does for enter-
tainment. Hot *Dog!* Why, even my own mother had
a Number 23 Joe Viola baseball card, which sat on a
shelf in the den in a red plastic heart-shaped frame,
right beside a picture of the Pope.

Anyway, Winky was a super-fan, even now that
he could barely see. "Baseball is all about connecting," he says. "The eye and the ball and the bat and
the heart."

"Maybe Viola's not as wonderful as you say he

is," I said. When he gets riled up, Winky's hair really punctuates.

"You take that back." Winky stuffed a fist under each armpit, probably to keep from reaching across the table and strangling me. "There is no player as great as Joe Viola."

"Mmm-hmm." I knew the next part by heart, so I said it: "Gives away his money, hole in his heart, charity machine . . ."

Winky kept speechifying right over me. "Joe Viola was born with a *hole in his heart*. He overcame his birth defect and became a great player. And he makes a ton of money for charity, too. All he has to do is *show up*." With that, Winky pointed energetically at the ceiling, as if Joe Viola might be floating around up there like the Ghost of Christmas Past. (That is a reference to author Charles Dickens, who Mr. Mee keeps telling me to read.) "Car wash, fancy dinner, cocktail party, talent show, the money rolls in." He put his hands together like a person praying. "I won't say I'm not concerned about him losing his touch. But it's temporary. I have faith."

Winky has had lots of practice testing his faith. For the past six or seven months, his father had found the balding corduroy couch in the Wheatons' front room a nice change from the job he lost at Sebago-Look Shoe Mill, and his mother suffered from diverticulitis. Her doctor said her condition was not serious, but she believed it to be and in that case what's the difference?

And then there's the legal blindness, of course. Basically, if Winky looked straight at me from the other side of the table, he could see my hair around the edges, but he couldn't see my face in the middle. He didn't need a white cane or, too bad, a seeing-eye dog. A dog at school? That would be wicked.

He used to see fine. He used to play baseball and watch baseball on TV and go to the games at Hot Dogs Field, live, breathe, eat, and drink baseball. Everything changed when he started to lose his eyesight at eight years old. Some days are better than others, but generally his vision gets worse and worse as time goes by. Maybe he'll get that seeing-eye dog after all!

"I had my dream again," he was saying.

"Yeah? The one with you and the ball and the glove and the amazing catch?" (Winky even sleeps baseball.) Wink hadn't caught a ball since the second grade, but I didn't have to tell *him* that. "That would be a miracle," I said anyway.

"Yeah," Winky said. "If only."

He'd been having this same dream forever. In the dream, he was always a Major League Baseball player. He hits one outta the park and the fans go nuts. But nothing about Winky's dream could ever come true.

Believe me, I can relate to that. Every night when I was little, Mom used to tell me a story about Amanda "Mandy" Mandolin, a made-up girl who traveled widely and had many adventures and mishaps. Mandy was above-average brave and smart. The stories all had happy endings. I dream all the time about Amanda Mandolin, and those dreams, also, can never come true.

"Finish up, children, no loitering!" said Mrs. Blyth-Barrow. "This is elementary school, not a bistro on the French Riviera!" She has a phlegmy rumble to her voice that makes me need to clear my throat. Everyone knew that old Mrs. B-B, widowed young, lived in an apartment over Kenerson's Five and Ten in the company of several cats. Nobody knew how many.

Winky sat there loitering like a French person. "My dad says all of life is if-onlys," he said, about our dreams, I guess. "Ifs, mights, too-bads, and buts."

"You said butts," said Bubba Davis, who just then tractored between the tables in his big green sweatshirt like a big John Deere and gave Winky's head a shove while he was at it. Meanwhile, Becky Schenck spilled her water on my head.

"Hey!" I said, very reasonable.

"Becky!" rumbled Mrs. B-B.

"He bumped my tray!" She pointed at Bubba. Mrs. B-B turned her attention to Bubba, and Becky said, just to me and my wet head, "'Bout *time* you took a shower, Brillo." She shot a look at Winky and made a kiss-face she knew he couldn't see. "Has it ever occurred to you that Winky, here, would never sit with you in a million trillion zillion years if he could *see* you, Brillo?"

Becky slunk away like the weasel she is, and Winky, while ignoring Becky very thoroughly, passed me a paper napkin.

"Don't listen to her," Winky said. "You look good to me. Your hair is very recognizable."

Grandpa, Explained

Winky and I hustled to homeroom, where Mrs. Blyth-Barrow stood like a palace guard at the door. Her handbag was on the floor beside her desk, big as a house. I wondered how much money was in it. It was definitely large enough to stash a hundred and three dollars and eighty-seven cents.

That made me think of Grandpa. Let me tell you, as grandpas go, mine is wicked awesome. He looks like Yertle the Turtle. He used to have a highly successful business fixing up old houses. His business card said *A+ HOME WORK: We Get the Job Done Right*. One of his houses was even written up across six pages' worth of *Yankee Delight* magazine, November 1963. Then there was some problem or other with building permits, and after that the printing on his business card just said *Home Work*: *We Get the Job Done.* Then it said: *We Do Odd Jobs*.

As an example, there was the time Mrs. Blyth-Barrow hired Grandpa to hang a door to the hallway between the kitchen and the living room of her apartment. When she got home, the hallway was missing. In its place was something everybody secretly wants but nobody *has* except for spies, eccentric uncles, and wizard-types, and also which there is one of in the coolest castle ever, which is in Romania, and which I read about in *Ripley's Believe It or Not! Royal Edition.* Totally wicked.

Grandpa's door was not so much a door as it was a bookcase. I stared. Mrs. Blyth-Barrow stared. Grandpa beamed, very confident, like a lighthouse. He gave the bookcase a light tug, and when he did, another one of Grandpa's plaques came into view in my mind: *Way Will Open.*

"That is so wicked!" and "Absolutely not!" and "Haven't you always wanted a hidden-passage-swingaway-bookcase?" we all three said at once.

Mrs. Blyth-Barrow crossed her arms and generally looked like a person who had definitely not read about any castles in Romania whatsoever.

Grandpa lowered his eyes and made a prince-type move with his hand and wrist. "Consider it a gift, Mrs. Blith-Biffle. Mrs. Blithel-Bliff. Mrs.—"

"Oh for Pete's sake," said Mrs. Blyth-Barrow, "call me Balithia."

That didn't seem to help; Grandpa opened his mouth and, after a second, closed it again.

Inside, the bookcase was even better. The hallway was lit up by four wall sconces that looked like real candles—the bulbs were even flickering on purpose, not because they were about to burn out. A couple of cats wandered out and Mrs. B-B blinked, maybe because the walls were the color of Fleischmann's margarine. She sighed a big long sigh, maybe because of the paint fumes. She planted her fists on her hips just like at school when she would call on Bubba Davis and he'd burp the whole answer and it wasn't even correct.

"I suppose it will do," Mrs. B-B finally said. Her voice went all weary and droopy, but her face told a different story.

Which is why my mind went *here*:

One time when I was a little girl, Mrs. Bean next door? Her front yard exploded. One minute the grass was prickled all over with green spikes, and the next minute—*kapow!* Yellow daffodils everywhere. If there was one thing my mom liked, it was daffodils. So I went and got my little green-handled scissors and I lopped off every single daffodil to give to Mom. Mrs. Bean ran out of her house screaming Stop, You Little Vandal!, and Mom ran out of our house screaming What on Earth Is the Matter!, and when Mom saw me and the flowers and the big vein throbbing in Mrs. Bean's neck, well, she gave me a look. A wicked long look.

The very same look Mrs. Blyth-Barrow leveled at Grandpa.

And *that's* why I thought Mrs. Blyth-Barrow was about to kiss Grandpa's cheek. I thought she might whisper in his ear these words that my mom whispered in mine: "How is it that a little girl like you can take care of me? How is it possible that everything I need is here in your small hands?"

That memory is full of importance, like a TV After-School Special in my brain. Yellow flowers, yellow hair, yellow dress. Mom's breath was warm on my ear, and her kiss was soft as snowflakes on my cheek. A shiver started slowly around my feet and picked up speed along my backbone to my head, and my body felt like it was growing bigger. I'm telling you, that shiver felt like *goodness*. That shiver told me *I* was good. Suddenly I knew the magical formula for *being good*: all I had to do was take care of Mom!

However, that day back in Mrs. Blyth-Barrow's

apartment over the Five and Ten, Mrs. B-B did not whisper, and she did not kiss Grandpa's cheek. "Honestly, Mr. Bloom," she said instead, and pretty loud. "Your business card might as well say *We Do Jobs Oddly!*"

"Psssst. Josie!" Winky was hissing at me and I noticed my name hanging loudly in the air as if someone had just hollered it three or four times.

"Here!" I shouted.

By the way, Mom made me help Mrs. Bean around the yard for *three months*!

The Book of Knowledge

Every librarian will tell you that if you want answers, read. Hungry to know how to make macaroni and cheese? Read the box. Need to know how fast lightning travels? Read *Ripley's Believe It or Not!* (220,000 miles per hour, FYI.) Want to know about mortgages, bank fees, and home finances? Me neither, but I didn't have any choice.

After homeroom we had library. There are posters all over the library walls, with sayings on them and pictures of famous people. *Without education, you're not going anywhere in this world.* —Malcolm X. *Always remember that you are absolutely unique. Just like everyone else.* —Margaret Mead. Mr. Mee had not tacked up anything dumb like *Don't forget to floss.*

"Good morning, good morning." Mr. Mee hailed us that day (and every day) with his arms up in the air like a gospel singer going Hallelujah. He has heavy black-framed eyeglasses and a mustache, and he nearly always wears a white button-up shirt and a skinny black necktie and a zip-up sweater straight out of Mr. Rogers's closet. Mr. Mee was born in Bermuda and came to Maine for boarding school, way back when. He is something like fifty years old at this point, so people consider him a true Maineiac.

Becky Schenck moved out of Mr. Mee's range just so she could mouth at me, "You smell." Then she flipped her perfect blond hair and pinched her perfect little nose.

"Anything I can help you fine young people with today?" Mr. Mee asked us. He still has a little something of an accent, from Bermuda. I think you would call it a musical lilt because some of his syllables go *up* or *down* where you might think they wouldn't, the way sometimes words change a little to fit the music in a song. "Heinous homework?" said Mr. Mee. "Arduous assignment? Intriguing investigation?"

"No, thank you," I said, totally ignoring Becky, who was pretending to gag, by tilting my head and reading the spines on the closest shelf: NEW ARRIVALS. "Nothing particular." I didn't want him to know about the mortgage problem because everyone knows it isn't polite to talk about family money problems in public. "Just something to read. Maybe a magazine."

"Excellent, excellent," said Mr. Mee. "You have come to the right place, but see here!" Mr. Mee raised a finger. Then he turned around and got a big giant book, which he plopped on the desk. It was so heavy that it went *thud* and so old that it gave off a puff of dust. Winky sneezed.

"God bless," said Mr. Mee, and "Shh!" said Becky Schenck.

"This is the venerable *Children's Encyclopedia of Knowledge*," Mr. Mee said. He knocked his knuckles on the red cover. Gold writing made me figure it was expensive. I could probably sell it for a hundred and three dollars and eighty-seven cents.

"It's a book full of fantastic facts and fancy findings!" Mr. Mee said. He was staring at us over his eyeglasses. "And so imagine my surprise," he went on.

The clock above the door clicked. "Yes?" I said. Click. "Your surprise . . . ?"

Mr. Mee bent an eyebrow. "In this volume," he said, "I have found a number of falsehoods."

"Falsehoods," repeated Winky. He blinked a bunch. "In an encyclopedia?"

"Things once believed to be true," said Mr. Mee, "but—what with the passage of time, technological advances, etceteras—discovered to be false."

"Lies!" I said.

Mr. Mee shook his head. "Not lies, Josephine." He tapped a fingertip on the cover of the book. "There are things in this book that once were as good as true, but have since been proved to be, shall we say, not actual."

"Like the Tooth Fairy," said Winky.

Mr. Mee whipped his head so fast I felt a breeze. "Not at all," said Mr. Mee. "Our belief in things unproved is different. To my knowledge, nobody has proved that the Tooth Fairy does not exist."

"Never visited me," Winky said.

"What do you do with all your baby teeth?" I said.

"I keep 'em in a Band-Aids tin. Sometimes I rattle them around."

Mr. Mee cocked his head, maybe to listen in his mind's ear to the rattling of Winky's teeth. Then he opened the book and turned some pages. "Listen," he said after a little while. "The earth was once part of the sun that fell off," he read. He took off his glasses and rubbed his eyes. "Think of the poor fellow, the scientist, who'd believed the falsehood all along." Mr. Mee shook his head and his eyes went all misty like someone with a lot of regrets, on TV. "Everything he thought he knew about the ground beneath his feet. Not so."

I thought about that. Poor ye olde scientist. That must've been a wicked rough day.

"Did you know," said Bubba Davis, looking at us one by one, "that the Great Pyramid of Giza was built by aliens?"

Becky Schenck heaved a stack of books onto the desk and flipped her long, straight, blond hair over her shoulder. "Yoo-hoo, checking out books here," she whispered at the top of her lungs, as if Mr. Mee was her personal servant. Wicked rude.

Mr. Mee closed the *Children's Encyclopedia of Knowledge* and smiled at Becky. "Certainly, certainly." He stamped her books. "Excellent choices."

"What about you, Josephine?" said Mr. Mee. Becky moved on, throwing me a dirty look for her own mysterious Becky-reasons. "I always enjoy knowing your selections."

I usually would check out magazines, or my one favorite book, *Ripley's Believe It or Not!* or something a lot like it. So Mr. Mee did not bat an eye when he stamped *The VERY Best of Ripley's Believe It or Not!* on the counter.

Then I plopped another book on the counter, which I'd found on the New Arrivals shelf. On the cover was a kid surrounded by bricks of gold. The kid looked wicked satisfied. His hands were on his belly as if he'd just eaten one of the gold bricks. That kid probably never had to worry about paying the mortgage.

Without saying one word, Mr. Mee stamped *Child Millionaire: A Young Person's Guide to the Stock Market.* He closed the cover and pushed my books across the counter. Then he said, "You might consider reading more fiction. A good novel can prepare us for what might come our way in life. Fiction provides a safe place to contemplate our choices and weigh our decisions. And many times, you'll find a happy ending."

"Well, I like things that are *stranger* than fiction," I said. I scooped up my books. "Also, I thought school librarians weren't supposed to judge," I added.

Mr. Mee ignored that. "Give Dickens a try sometime," he said.

Mrs. Blyth-Barrow's Agenda

W hat the dickens," said Mrs. Blyth-Barrow.

We were sitting in Mrs. B-B's classroom after school the next day in a little ring of student chairs. She has very yellow hair that looks like you could knock on it, sort of a Darth Vader–type look if he wasn't on the Dark Side.

"To what are you referring, Mrs. Bith-Blith— Mrs., uh, Berth-Bith . . ." Grandpa always sat up wicked straight and talked fancy, very proper, when he was in these meetings with my teacher, as if she was *his* teacher too.

Mrs. B-B waved a hand, probably to make him stop hacking away at her name. "Let me begin by

saying that *ennui* is not a proper state for a child,"
Mrs. B-B said.

"Sir, yes sir!" Grandpa agreed. He stood and
saluted, for emphasis.

Mrs. B-B looked flattered.

Grandpa sat.

I raised my pointer finger. "*On-wee—*"

"Don't interrupt, Josie," Mrs. B-B interrupted.
"I recall my youth in Entwistle, where I was a girl
with a bright future, all the world ahead of me, and
every reason to enjoy all the confidence in the world."

What was she talking about? Hadn't she called
this meeting to talk about my grades again? I looked
at Grandpa for help, but by his dreamy face I could
tell he'd been carried away to Mrs. Blyth-Barrow's
youth in Entwistle, wherever that was.

"But—"

"Why don't you *apply* yourself, Josephine?"
she said, switching gears. That was more like it!
She leaned in. "You don't seem to care about your
grades, Josie"—she held up a hand—*no buts!*—as
if!—"but it may surprise you to know that I don't
care about your grades either."

That *was* a surprise. I looked at Grandpa. He
looked at me. We were like a couple of bunny rab-
bits caught out in the open.

"What I *do* care about is that you *try*," she said, "and that you *learn*. Something. Anything."

Without moving my head, I sliiiiiiid my eyes upward from Mrs. B-B's hard yellow hair to the clock, but the hands hadn't moved. Then I rolled my eyeballs sideways to look out the windows. It was a nice day. Hamburg is especially nice during that week or so in spring when the mud season is nearly over and the black fly season hasn't come on yet. I realized that the only way to get from in here in this stuffy classroom to out there in the nice day was to agree with whatever my teacher said.

"Tryyyy," I said, nodding. "I'll try that."

Mrs. B-B sat back in her chair and smiled.

I do try, I thought. Just not that often or much. Winky's more of a try-er.

Grandpa sat back in his chair, like Mrs. B-B, and smacked his hands on his thighs. "We seem to be having a fine conversation here. I would add, as a wise man once said, it is better to remain silent and be thought a fool than to speak and remove all doubt."

Grandpa's motto had about as much to do with my homework or grades as Mrs. B-B's youth in Entwistle, as far as I could tell. It was one long blurt.

"I couldn't disagree more, Mr. Bloom," said Mrs. B-B. Her hair bobbed side to side.

This was interesting. Grandpa's motto challenged? I looked from one to the other. The clock hands moved a little.

Suddenly Mrs. B-B leaned forward. Her hair swung like the Liberty Bell. "Do you even possess a hairbrush?"

Hey! Well, I couldn't get a brush through my hair even if I had one.

"No offense," she went on. "I'm sure you're doing a fine job caring for Josephine . . ."

What?

"Cheese and rice!" Grandpa said.

I sat wicked still, so as to seem like I hadn't noticed Grandpa's blurting. Did Mrs. B-B notice it? I wasn't exactly sure why I didn't want her to notice, except that the blurting seemed . . . new and unusual. I didn't want to see Grandpa's business card go from *Odd Jobs* to just . . . *Odd*!

I didn't need to worry, because Mrs. Blyth-Barrow had what she liked to call during morning meeting her *agenda*. And her agenda was me. "But isn't she a bit, err, rough around the edges, hmm? A bit unkempt? A bit, shall we sayyy . . . unnn-hygienic?"

Come on, now, she made up that word.

She folded her hands in her lap. "A feminine influence is in order. Wouldn't you agree, Mr. Bloom?"

What what *what*? Mrs. B-B's meeting was taking more turns than an episode of *The Sands of Time*! It's a show about a sprawling family of cattle ranchers, the Sands, who live in a quaint town in Texas called Time. Time has got everything a drama needs in the way of shops and businesses and interesting inhabitants, plus good-looking visitors are always moving in. You can hardly believe what goes on there, but I guess that's the point.

Anyway, it's true that my Toughskins had grass stains, but what you do with blue jeans is, you give them a good shake before you put them on again. And I'd taken a bath just two days before. Two days? Maybe four days. I couldn't remember *exactly*. I sniffed in the direction of my right armpit. No problems. I also checked my breath by blowing on my hand and smelling. Smelled fine. Like breath.

"Well, well, that's all very well," Grandpa said. He frowned at me. What did *I* do?

"No advice columnist for any newspaper in the world would tell you otherwise, and I would know," said Mrs. B-B. "For seven long and intensely dull months I was 'Dear Beth,' for the *Punxsutawney Daily Shadow*, yes, *that* Punxsutawney. The editor-in-chief believed no one would write to a Dear Balithia. I can tell you that in Punxsutawney, anyway, people are all the same. Their problems boil down to one thing: communication!"

"Talk is cheap," said Grandpa.

"Silence is costly," said Mrs. B-B.

Grandpa had the last word. "Waffles!"

Mrs. B-B blinked like an owl on *Animal Kingdom*. But then she kind of twinkled, like a mom in a peanut butter ad. "Oh my, Mr. Bloom. The wit! The *leaps* of brain power!" She turned to me. "Am I right?" She actually seemed to want to know. Probably she was trying to decide if Grandpa was showing *leaps* of brain power, or a *shortage* of brain power. I'd seen her look at me the same way in math class.

So I said, "Right!" with all the confidence of a youth in Entwistle.

She landed on the side of *leap*. "One can hardly keep up!" she said.

I had no trouble keeping up with that one. It followed that this talk of things being cheap and costly made Grandpa remember the waffles at Moody's Diner, which had gone up in price and down in quality since Mrs. Beverly Moody retired and her granddaughter Debbie Moody-Cote took over. I, myself, had been ordering the pancakes instead.

Mrs. B-B stood up, so we did too. Then she

said, "This child needs to bathe." Wicked abrupt!

"I do bathe!" I said.

"Regularly."

"All right already!"

"In the bathtub."

"Where else?"

"With soap."

"I know that!" Geez! I looked at Grandpa, but he was drumming his fingers together and making a sort of humming noise and sidling toward the door.

"*Mis*-ter Bloom!" said Mrs. B-B. He stopped mid-sidle. "There are items a girl needs that a grandfather might not think of having in the house. Feminine items."

"Got it!" he said. His face was glowing about as bright as his blaze-orange hunting cap.

"There is no need for embarrassment. *Mennnstroooaaation* is perfuhhllyy waaaahh garble bidddlle prrrr gggaahhh."

I'd stopped hearing anything after the word "menstruation," the absolute worst word of all time, especially from your *teacher* with your *grand*father standing right there! "Mrs. B-B! I mean—I'm not—I don't need those things, Mrs. Blyth-Barrow!" my voice sounded as blaze-orange as Grandpa's face. Where was a giant, person-size

Brenda's Book Cozy when you needed one to wrap yourself in?

"But you will need them," she said, her voice all quiet and creepy, "and you will need other things too. Someone to talk to." As if I'd talk to my *teacher* about . . . about anything! "I am here for you, Josephine. And I am here for you, Mr. Bloom. And I am paying attention. If all aspects of this child's care are not attended to, I will notice. And I will take steps."

Steps? What steps? Did she know about the mortgage and the water and the lights? And even though she was using a soft voice, why did it sound like Grandpa and I were both being sent to the principal's office?

The Not-Secret Fort

On Saturday, someone came and planted a FOR SALE sign on the next-door neighbors' front yard.

"Why would the Beans want to leave Hamburg?" I asked Grandpa. Had Mr. and Mrs. Bean not paid their mortgage? Would we have to sell our house too? Five days had gone by since I'd found that mortgage statement, and so far all I'd done about it was sneak around the house looking for some more of Grandpa's fishy money.

Grandpa glanced up from what he was doing, which was arranging a bunch of peanuts-in-the-shell on the mudroom steps.

"Hidey-hole!" Grandpa blurted. Then he said,

"Pete lost his job. Cutbacks at the paper mill. They're moving away to live with their grown-up daughter over to Portland, so she can help in their declining years."

"Why doesn't she move over here and live with them?"

Grandpa set down another peanut. "Because they're old farts."

I thought about that.

"There comes a point, Josie," Grandpa went on, "when old people get treated like children." He cracked open a peanut. "At least Pete and Vera have each other to complain to." He popped the peanuts in his mouth and stared at the FOR SALE sign, chewing and chewing. Thoughtful, like a cow.

I stared at the FOR SALE sign too. "Can I have a peanut?"

I said it again, to Winky this time. "I don't know why anybody would want to leave Hamburg." I handed him two of the four peanuts Grandpa had been willing to part with. We were in the backyard of Unexpected House, which was the *front* yard of our secret fort. "Hamburg has the longest single-span bridge in the United States." I remembered this from the Get Local! unit in social studies.

"Longest in New England, and not anymore,"

said Winky. He set aside his digging stick so he could crack the peanuts. We had an idea we'd plant a little patch of garden for our fort, and the first step to most goals is always the digging.

I also remembered another fact: at one time not so very long ago, Hamburg produced more broom handles and paper and shoes than any other town. So I said that, too.

Winky didn't say anything, so I guess I was right about that.

The next-door neighbors' was not the only house for sale in Hamburg. There were three others, not counting Unexpected House, which had been for sale since third grade, probably because it's not regular. A regular house has four sides and a roof, for one thing. Unexpected House is a geodesic dome. It looks like an Eskimo igloo. It's even painted icy blue. It's three doors up from Winky's house on Flint Street. We call Flint Street "Desirable Street" because that's what it said on the real estate flyer:

Unexpected House on Desirable Street!

Every so often somebody would come and take out the old flyers from the box on the signpost and put in new ones that were nearly the same except for the price, which got smaller, and the description, which got bigger. *Special Opportunity!* was a new one that Saturday, for example. So was *As-is!*

Could Be Charming! And *Must-see—Looks Larger Inside!*

The backyard was grown over with the kind of scrubby weeds that Grandpa would call a fire hazard. There is a weeping willow tree at the very back of the yard. The long hair of the tree reaches all the way to the ground, all around. And behind that curtain was our secret fort. From the outside, nobody even knew it was there. It was all ours for the trespassing. Wicked!

I was thinking about people moving, and about when Winky moved to Hamburg so his dad could work at Sebago-Look Shoe Mill. He blinked a lot and wore a baseball glove at all times, and Becky Schenck and them all said he was weird.

"You know what, Winky?" I said.

"What."

"I never told you, but that first day, when you came to school in second grade? Mrs. Crosier made me sit with you because she said you had special promise and needed a caring helper."

"Huh," Winky said. "She said the same thing to me. About sitting next to you."

"She did?" I said. "Special promise?"

"Yup."

"Caring helper?"

"Yup."

We both dug in the dirt a little while with our digging sticks.

Digging and wondering are what they call natural companions. I dug and I wondered . . . It's true that Winky's my best friend, and also he is pretty much my only friend. But was the reason we were friends because . . . nobody else would want us? Because . . . we were a couple of real losers?

I stabbed at my thoughts and the dirt with my digging stick. *Stab-stab-stab.* I nearly stabbed a little acorn with a tiny sprout.

"Look at this cute little guy," I said to Winky.

While Winky studied the acorn with his magnifier, I had a thought that stunned me. It stunned me so much I thought it out loud, and loudly: "Winky!" I said. "The whole, entire tree is inside that nut."

Winky said, "Huh."

I sat back on my heels and hugged my knees. My acorn-thought was making me happy and smiley. I put my thought another way: "The nut is the little heart of the tree."

"That's neat," Winky said, agreeable.

We planted the little acorn in the ground and spent some time surrounding it with a little fence of twigs. Maybe someday a big tree would grow.

I added another twig to the tiny fence.

Or maybe, I thought, we weren't that good at

being gardeners, and the little tree would dry up and die. Maybe we weren't going to be able to keep it safe from squirrels. Maybe we weren't that good, period.

I poked Wink's arm with my digger. "Are we real . . . lo—" I didn't want to say *loser* out loud.

"Lucky?" Winky said. He grinned. "Yep. We sure are. Wicked lucky! If Mrs. Crosier hadn't put us together, well, who knows what."

I went back to digging. I felt better. Two friends planting a baby tree. What could have more special promise than that?

After a while Winky went into the fort to get us a drink from the fridge. The fridge was actually an old Coleman cooler, which we used for keeping cookies and soda when we can get it.

"Josie, come in here!" Winky hollered.

I walked over and parted the willow hair and went in. And there, in our secret fort, was a beautiful but alarming thing: the cooler was filled to the top with all kinds of good food: apples and oranges, a jar of peanut butter, saltine crackers, Li'l Smokies beef jerky sticks. There were beautiful chocolate bars with pictures of little German boys and girls in lederhosen and whatnot on the wrappers. There were tiny cans of pineapple juice "fresh from Hawaii." There were gumdrops in all the colors. I love gumdrops. The fridge looked just like a Christmas display at the Pay 'n Takit.

I looked at Winky. Winky dropped his magnifying glass and looked at me. We both looked at all the food that had magically appeared in our secret fort, and we were both thinking the same thing:

Someone knows.

A Carnival

Once we got over the shock of our secret fort being not-secret, there was nothing to do but get over it. Why? Because we were hungry, and there was all that food.

"Unless—unless it's poisoned," I said. Boy those chocolate bars looked good. "Or there could be razor blades in those apples," I added.

Winky raised his magnifier and studied everything that was in the cooler. Then he picked up one of the apples and bravely took a bite.

"Nope," he said. "Good apple."

That was all I needed to hear. "Well, this is my kind of mystery," I said. I was right about the chocolate.

We ate till we were stuffed, and we didn't even get to the bottom of the cooler. Everything was nice and peaceful. We went back to digging. Then Winky had to go and ruin it.

"What about a dunk tank?" said Winky.

"What *about* a dunk tank?"

"You know, to make money and pay the mortgage."

Oh yeah, the mortgage. It had been so nice, forgetting all about the one hundred and three dollars and eighty-seven cents for two whole seconds. But Winky was right.

Days left to get the money: ten.

Ideas for getting the money: zero.

"It's too chilly for a dunk tank," I said. I found an old Popsicle stick from way last summer in my sweatshirt pocket, and I stuck it in the ground beside the other little twigs in a ring around the tiny sprout. Maybe a big tree would grow.

"Maybe we'll find buried treasure, right here," Winky said. "That really would be unexpected."

"Also, it would be stealing," I said.

"Yeah. I guess." Winky dragged his stick around and made an *X* in the dirt. "Hey, what about people pay us to put on their little kids' birthday parties?" he said.

"We'd have to wait for somebody's birthday. We need something we can do right now."

"What about a carnival?"

A carnival was a great idea. I could just about feel the money in my pocket already. "Wicked."

It wasn't a carnival, so much as a single game. It turns out a carnival is really hard work for two people. We spent most of Saturday planning, and all we came up with was a ball-toss.

Sunday morning was mild and sunny, more than half-decent for March. I set a bunch of empty cut-off milk cartons all in a row in the parking lot of the House of Harmony Church and waited for Winky to come out the big doors. Grandpa never took me to church. He said Grandma used to drag him to Sunday service, and when she went to heaven, he never had to go to church anymore, and that was the one good thing about her passing. When he said this, he sounded wicked crabby. A get-out-of-church-free pass was a very poor prize, considering. Anyway, we planned on snaring the after-service, pre-coffee business of generous church-type folk.

Each contestant stood at a chalk line, and tossed a baseball, trying to land a ball in a carton. At first it was too easy and we had to give

out a prize right off the bat. (We'd bought a bag
of balloons, and when some little Sunday school
kid got a ball in, Winky blew up a balloon and
tied a length of string to it and handed it to her.
She walked away dragging the balloon behind her
bump . . . bump . . . bump and I have to say it looked
pretty sad.)

After that we drew the line a lot farther away.

"What are you kids raising money for?" asked
Reverend Smith. I did not want to talk about me
paying the mortgage. Everybody knows it's inap-
propriate to discuss family finances in public. Also,
here came Mrs. Blyth-Barrow across the parking
lot. After that weird meeting we'd had, I didn't want
her to pay me too much attention. Even though I
had been washing my face every night hard enough
to scrub all the freckles off, and even though I'd
been trying to work out the knots in my hair, she
still might "take steps."

"Charity-*college*." Winky and I spoke as one,
but different words.

We looked at each other.

"Church," I said, and Winky said, "Children." I
elbowed him.

"*Blind* children," he said, putting on just the
right pathetic touch, I thought.

Everything was going well, and we hadn't had

to give out any more sad balloons, when the game drew what I think they call in the carnival business, first blood.

Bubba Davis was at the line, and instead of tossing the baseball underhand, all reasonable, he let loose a slurve. Maybe it was a two-seamed fastball. Some kind of fast, hard throw, anyway, right when Becky Schenck happened to cross behind the cartons sing-songing at me, "He-ey, Bril—"

Whack!

Becky's hands flew to her face and she started screaming.

Mrs. B-B thundered up. "Violence," she said, shooting a look at me, "is never the answer."

"She walked in front of the ball!" I said.

Mrs. B-B tut-tutted and tossed her head. Her yellow hair crested like a wave on a rough day at Pickerel Pond.

"Gaaha," Becky groaned.

Mrs. B-B's hair ebbed. "Becckkhkky," she gargled, "let's get you inside the parish hall at once and see to"—she curled her lip at the gooey blood beneath Becky's nostrils and circled her hand before her face—"that business."

Becky Schenck moaned again.

Winky stuck his face a little too close to Becky's in order to eyeball the injury. Becky hissed

"Tsssgitawayyy," flapped her bloodied hands, and drew back her neck like a Canada goose.

Mrs. B-B put an arm around Becky Schenck's shoulders and started to walk her away. "There, there, Becky," she said, nice and soothing. "Your nose will never be the same. I once worked as a scout for a modeling agency, so I should know. Head up and away, dear," she added, "this sweater is angora-blend. And you, Josephine Bloom!" She shot back over her shoulder, "I'll be calling a meeting, you can count on that!" before turning back to Becky. "Angora-blend, Becky. Gahh! Angora-blend!"

After that, Winky and I packed up the game and counted our money. Seven dollars, minus the balloons, and we'd probably have to give it to Mrs. Blyth-Barrow to pay for her dry cleaning.

Yard Work

Then Winky had another idea. "What about we go door-to-door and do spring cleanups?" We got a wheelbarrow from the garage, and two rakes and a push broom, and it only took four doors till we got our first customer, Dr. Wilmer, DMD.

We worked hard for an hour. We raked every last rotten leaf on the ground, and pulled up every last green weed. When we were finished, you could see the nice neat lines of our rakes in the dirt, and there wasn't a green thing left on the property. We even yanked up a whole big clump of tangled greenery under a birch tree. Dr. Wilmer came out to check our work. He looked all around, real slow. His mouth kind of gaped open, like when you are very impressed with everything you are seeing, you can hardly believe it! It took him a couple tries to get any words out, but when he did, he said, "Oh, my pachysandras terminalus!"

I looked around the yard proudly. "I'll say!" I said.

Then Dr. Wilmer opened up his wallet. "Here's four dollars never to clean up my yard again," he said. Then he kind of staggered back into his house. His feet kicked up all the freshly turned dirt where we'd got rid of all the ugly weeds.

"What does 'pachysandras terminalus' mean?" Winky asked me.

"Beats me!" I said.

At the end of the day we had twenty dollars even, counting the carnival money plus Dr. Wilmer's four dollars, two dollars each from Mrs. Moody-Cote from the diner and Mr. Grigg, the postman. Mr. Miller at the Pay 'n Takit had paid us five dollars to wash the store's plate glass windows, inside and out. I gave Winky half the money, but he gave it back because he said on a scale of one to ten, a kid saving up to pay the mortgage is a ten, and a blind kid saving up for a Boston Believers' game his parents won't even *let* him go to is only about a one. I didn't *want* to agree with him, but I kept all the money just the same.

The Shape of Longing

On Monday, Mrs. Blyth-Barrow and Mr. Mee team-taught a poetry unit in the library. A lot of kids groaned like this: "Not poe-eh-treeeeeeee!" as if what they meant was "Not *death* by poe-eh-treeeee!"

It was Bubba Davis's turn to read aloud. "IthinkthatIshallneversee, apoemaslovelyasatree."

Mrs. B-B frowned. "Slowly, Bubba, please. *Enjoy* the words. Enjoy!" She made a wheel-motion with her hand that meant "Once more, from the top."

Bubba sighed. "I . . . think . . . that . . . I . . . shall . . . never . . . see . . . a . . . poem . . . as . . . lovely . . . as . . . a . . . tree."

I woke up when my chin hit my chest.

Mr. Mee cleared his throat. "Thank you, Bubba, for that recitation of Mr. Frost's poem. I think we can all agree, poetry excites the imagination!"

It was quiet. I guess nobody agreed.

"Now it's time to write our own poems," said Mr. Mee. He was standing beside an easel with a big pad on it. He picked up a Sharpie and uncapped it with a flourish. "Observe!" he said.

He turned to the easel and wrote:

> *Mountains toppling evermore*
> *Into seas without a shore;*
> *Seas that restlessly aspire,*
> *Surging, unto skies of fire;*
> *Lakes that endlessly outspread*
> *Their lone waters—lone and dead—*
> *Their still waters—still and chilly*
> *With the snows of the lolling lily.*

The poem was going pretty well before the lolling lily part, in my opinion. But the neat thing was how Mr. Mee wrote out the poem on the pad. He stacked the words so they made the shape of a mountain. For the part about the lone waters, he made the words spread out from the base of the mountain on either side, so that the words made up the surface of the sea. When he was done writing the mountain in the sea, we all clapped.

"Thank you, thank you, and thanks *ad infinitum*, wouldn't you agree, to Edgar Allan Poe."

Crickets.

"Of course I've taken liberties with Mr. Poe's poem," Mr. Mee said, "excerpting certain lines, writing the words into a shape . . ." His voice drifted away, one might say, like ripples in lone waters.

Mr. Mee tapped the Sharpie on the easel. "To take the exercise further, I could write a new poem, my own poem, about something large and abstract. An idea or a condition. Let's say the idea or the condition is 'longing.' I could write my poem, as I did this one," he said, tapping the easel again, "in the shape of a mountain. Let's say my poem doesn't have the word 'mountain' in it at all, and yet the shape of the poem illustrates, amplifies, the very subject of the poem. One's longing might be said to be as large, as solid, as *profound*, as a mountain." Mr. Mee looked at us.

We looked up, down, left, and right.

"Do you understand?" said Mr. Mee.

Someone had to throw our librarian a life preserver, and it was me. "Yes," I said. Oh, I understood, all right. My longing was in the shape of a mountain too. A mountain of money.

You know how sometimes your brain jumps from one thought to another thought, and you're not sure how it got there? I mention this because right then my brain went from the word *profound* to: Heck, I have a dad that is probably not dead, and if he's not exactly *waiting* to be found, still, he must be out there for the finding, right? There was a character on *The Sands of Time* who didn't know he had a kid, and when he found out, he cried and cried—he was so happy to give away his vast fortune.

Anyone who's ever read a single chapter from *Ripley's* knows for a fact that truth is even stranger than fiction. If I had a dad out there . . . wouldn't he have to give me money?

The Bank

I put that thought about a rich dad in my back pocket, along with the twenty dollars Winky and I made over the weekend, and I went to the Anchor Bank.

I pushed my way through the revolving door and stood in line for the next available bank teller. There were two. One was nice Mrs. Gagne. The other was Mr. Beebe. I hoped I would get Mrs. Gagne when it was my turn at the counter.

The bank is an old brick building with tiny white-and-black honeycomb tiles on the floor, and a high ceiling with lights that dangle on chains longer than I am tall. I looked up and counted the lights. I looked down and counted tiny tiles. I read over the pamphlet from the tables in the back, the ones with pens on chains so nobody will take them. I read words like *deposit* and *withdrawal* and *saving for your future.* Then Mrs. Gagne called me over to her window.

"Hello, Josie," she said. She had pretty earrings about the size of the bank's chandeliers. "How may the Anchor be of service?" she said.

"I'd like to make a deposit to my grandfather's account," I said. "Is that . . . lawful?"

"Yes," she said, "making a deposit is perfectly lawful." I slid the money we'd made, all in single dollar bills, across the counter. I had saved a lot more in the Keds box under my bed for a rainy day, but this was a good experiment.

"Savings or checking?"

"Huh?"

A line formed behind me while Mrs. Gagne told me all about checkbooks and check stubs and keeping records of checks and how people use checks to pay their bills.

She told me about credits and debits, and how citizens record their credits and debits to be sure their spending is in line with their earnings.

"Check!" I said.

"Debits are your monthly expenses, utility

Not So Fast

All I had to do was find Grandpa's checkbook! I had already practiced Grandpa's signature from a couple of notes I'd written to get out of school, once because I'd had enough of Becky Schenck and I went to the cemetery and talked to Mom, and another time because I'd had enough of Becky Schenck and I went home and watched game shows. No more stuffing cash into envelopes. Paying the bills would be a piece of cake.

I ran down the driveway, and when I did, squirrels scattered every which-a-way, over the stone wall, up onto the picnic table, off behind the garage. There really were a good many squirrels. Through the open garage doors I could see Grandpa busy at bills and so on," she explained. As if *that* needed explaining!

"Credits are things like Social Security, pension, and income from other sources."

"Income from other sources—that sounds mysterious," I said.

"Yes," said Mrs. Gagne, "it can be a very forgiving category."

None of this helpful information was explained in that *Child Millionaire* book from the library, by the way.

Then Mrs. Gagne gave me a receipt. (Also a bright green lollipop out of the *For Our Little Piggybankers* bucket.) On the receipt was jotted: Account Balance: $314.42. Bingo!

I sucked on the lollipop all the way home, green-apple happy now that I knew how to pay all the bills out of all the money in Grandpa's bank account. I was practically a banking expert already! From now on, it would be easy: I'd just write checks. Wicked!

his workbench, sawing and banging and blurting.

I dropped my jacket on a kitchen chair and went into the den to Grandpa's secretary. I lowered the slanted panel that, once dropped, becomes the desktop part. I rooted around in the little drawers and slots, looking for a checkbook. I found a post-card from Big Deals Clearing House: *You May Be Our Next Big Deal! Watch for the Winner-Wagon!* I found some slips of paper with numbers on them. Maine State Lottery MEGA MOOLAH tickets from the Pay 'n Takit.

Then I saw an envelope with a return address that made me wonder. It's a federal offense to tamper with the US mail. The envelope was sealed, and it was not addressed to me. But that ship had sailed way back in January, so I criminally opened the envelope with barely a second thought. Inside was a color brochure and a letter from the new Downeast Best Rest Home for Retirement and Assisted Living on Route 4. It promised Dear Martin Bloom excellent care, a lively social life, and a nightly salad bar. One picture on the brochure was of a smiling nurse with a nametag: NANCY. Another one showed an old man and an old woman about to slosh their glasses of wine because of laughing their heads off. Another one was of some vegetables.

Why did Grandpa have this brochure?

I looked off into the distance, like people do on *The Sands of Time* when they're thinking about the future or the past or something else that's disturbing.

My eye landed on the photograph of Grandma Kaye in the silver frame on the shelf above Joe Viola and the Pope. In her photo she looks grim and gloomy, just like the Irish grandma in the canned beef stew commercial does *not*. Grandpa says I take after her, on account of I look Irish—her side of the family was the McPhee clan.

Right then her face made me feel guilty about going through Grandpa's secretary. And about opening his mail. And lying to him. And forging his signature. And hiding his money.

Then I thought, maybe me taking after Grandma Kaye, looks-wise, makes Grandpa miss her. Maybe I make him sad, that way. Or maybe he wants a new wife, not a possibly-stinky old granddaughter. Well. I would have to save that worry for another day.

I put the letter from Downeast Best Rest back in the secretary and opened up the little drawers until—wicked!—I found a checkbook.

A Family Portrait

By then it was near suppertime. I closed up the desk and went to pull the curtains, happy I'd solved our money problems. That was good. That was wicked. But my thoughts were as bouncy with question marks as Winky Wheaton's hair. Was Grandpa thinking about moving to the Downeast Best Rest? Did he want a social life and salad? Was Nancy a real nurse, or just an actor for the picture? Would the Winner-Wagon really come to our house?

There I went again, looking off into the future or the past or something. This time, my gaze crash-landed on the picture of me and Mom at a Hot Dogs game. In the picture, Mom had on a funny paper hat for selling hot dogs in the concession stand. Her blond ponytail was flipped forward over her shoulder like a fashion model. She looked like *Sporty Barbie Goes to the Baseball Game*.

I took up the picture from the shelf.

"Hi," I said to the picture. I touched my finger to the glass over Mom's face. Then I touched the spot where a dad would be.

As soon as I was able to wonder about fathers, I wanted to know where mine was. "Atlantic City is where we met," Mom told me. "I was only there on my way to somewhere else, but there he was. I very much do not know or *want* to know his permanent address."

But *I* wanted to know. And I wanted to know *who* he was.

"Oh, he was a real player, that guy, fairly famous," is how Mom described him. "Charming, handsome, and a first-class jerk. We married in a rush of love, Josie-honey. Soon I was pregnant with you! When I told him about the baby, he was so excited he grabbed his coat, ran out for champagne, and never came back."

And that would always be that. "End of story, Josie."

I squinted at the picture. There I was, three feet tall and looking not a thing like Sporty Barbie's Daughter. My hair was in two thick red braids, which Mom used to do. In the picture the braids were frizzed and the ends looked like old toothbrushes. My face was covered all over with freckles. If I inherited his looks, my dad must have looked more like Raggedy Andy than Sporty Ken.

Just then I heard Grandpa coming in the house. I set that picture back on the shelf, and shoved the checkbook in the back pocket of my Toughskins.

The very next day I wrote out a check to Red Flag Mortgage and dropped it in the mailbox on the corner of Pine and Maine. If only I had an address for a dad, I thought, I could send him a letter. But that was okay, perfectly okay, because now our money problems were over.

What's Insufficient Funds?

Our money problems were not over.

"What's 'insufficient funds'?" I asked Winky. I showed him the letter that came two weeks after from Red Flag Mortgage.

"Not enough money," Winky said. He let his magnifier fall back onto his stomach.

I guess I figured that, from the place where the letter had a "penalty fee," and an even bigger amount due than before.

We were meeting in the secret fort. I opened the fridge and pulled out a can of fruit punch. The Coleman cooler had been stocked up again, and since neither of us had dropped dead from eating the magically appearing food, we just kept eating it.

I learned from the pickle I was in with Red Flag Mortgage that just because you write a check doesn't mean the money is actually available to spend. Maybe Grandpa had taken money out of the bank account. Maybe he had written a check without marking it in what Mrs. Gagne had called "the check register." Maybe he put a dollar figure in the credit column when it should have gone in the debit column. For whatever mysterious and confusing reason, the money that was *in* the account the day I wrote the check, was *not* there to cover the check by the time it got to the offices of Red Flag Mortgage. That spoiled-rotten *Child Millionaire* kid from that book had none of these problems! Every time I turned around, somebody with a red stamp and a temper wanted money we didn't have.

"I learned about embezzlement on *The Sands of Time*," I told Winky. "Maybe Grandpa embezzled."

"You can't embezzle from your own bank account. That's just called spending."

"Well, what is Grandpa *spending* on, as you call it, if not to pay the bills?"

I asked Grandpa that very question that very night, and I don't know if his answer was a real one, or just a blurt:

"Peanuts!"

Soccer

 eanuts."

I kicked the soccer ball to Winky.

We were walking around Hamburg, passing a soccer ball back and forth so Winky could practice his vision. That's what he calls it, practicing his vision. He got a foot on the ball and kicked it back to me.

I trapped the ball and passed it back.

"I don't know," I said. "Sometimes the thing he blurts makes sense, pretty much, once you think on it."

"Over here!" came a shout across the recess field. It was the mailman. Winky kicked the soccer ball in Mr. Grigg's direction, but it went wide.

"I got it!" yelled Sandy from Dippin' Donuts. She must have been late for work because after she kicked the ball to Mr. Grigg, she kept on running in the direction of Maine Street and the ties of her pink bib apron were flapping behind her. Too bad because pretty soon we had a little game going, and that Sandy can really run.

"Hey!" hollered Mr. Grigg. Mrs. Blyth-Barrow stole the ball right out from under him and dribbled it fast away. She must have snuck up on him in her sensible shoes. It was wicked impressive. She dribbled it across the field and kicked it straight between the trash can and the water fountain.

"Gooooaaaalll!" shouted Mrs. B-B. She jumped up and down and pumped both fists in the air. Her hair stayed in place the whole time.

"Who said that's where the goal is?" I said to her.

"Clearly that's the goal," she said. I'm telling you, she wasn't even winded.

I elbowed Winky. "Is that the goal?"

"I call Mrs. B-B!" Winky said.

So I got Mr. Grigg for my team. Mr. Grigg is a reliable, friendly person, but he is not what anybody would call speedy. Also he was weighed down by the postal bag, which he refused to take off and drop on the ground. I asked politely, three times. I also got Grandpa when he showed up. I won't say I "got stuck with" Grandpa, but that is what I mean.

Then Chief Costello came by, walking his little yappy dog, Sparky. Sparky was not on one team or the other, but Chief Costello played on Winky's team to even up the sides.

The score was three to two when I saw a perfect shot to Grandpa to tie it up.

I kicked the ball to Grandpa, go, go, come on, *go*, and wouldn't you know he picked that moment to stop and take a good long look at his watch. "Gin rummy!" he blurted. He gave a sharp salute, turned on his heel, and let the ball roll right by.

"Grandpa! The game!" I hollered, but he was in a hurry, wherever he was going, and he didn't even look back. Everybody watched him go.

"That wasn't very sportsmanlike," I said.

"Well, neither snow nor rain nor soccer will keep me from my task," said Mr. Grigg. Too bad, I thought, since I knew that big sack always held bad news. Mrs. B-B tightened her shoe straps and walked off with what you might call gusto. We really needed some players under age fifty. What with jobs and oldness, it wasn't much of a game.

Thanks to Mrs. B-B and her Velcro-fastened orthopedic shoes, my team didn't stand a chance anyway. But I did not appreciate Grandpa abandoning me in the middle of the game. What was more important, and where was he going?

Plastic Flowers

We kicked the ball back and forth some more and ended up at the cemetery.

Winky Wheaton is the only person in the world who knows I sometimes go to the cemetery and talk to Mom. For one thing, it's private and personal, and only a best friend can be trusted with private and personal things. For another thing, I do something that might be slightly illegal, when I'm there. When I see old plastic flowers on some grave that nobody's visited for a long time, I take the ones that are still good, even though they were meant for some other dead person, and I rearrange them and put them on Mom's grave. In terms of grave robbing, it doesn't seem that bad.

So we did that. I shook out the pinchers and ants and slimy water and bunched the plastic flowers, mostly yellow, into a bouquet. I put the bouquet on Mom's grave.

"Fresh as a daisy," Winky said. He picked up the soccer ball and put it under his arm, out of respect, like a hat.

"We're having a little bit of money trouble, Mom," I said toward the gravestone, "but there's nothing to worry about. I've got it under control. I'm taking care of it."

"Do you ever hear anything back?" Winky whispered.

"No," I said. "Not so far." But I am ever-hopeful, just like those plastic flowers are ever-blooming.

A Bet with Mr. Mee

About a week went by. The Believers were back home in Boston for the start of the regular season, and the Hamburg Hot Dogs' Opening Day came and went. Opening Day was always the first Saturday of April, even if it snowed. The whole town was there. If I was smart, I'd have taken the opportunity to rob a few houses while everybody was at the game. But I didn't, and the mortgage was due the next week. Again.

"Josephine, can you tell me what the highest mountain is?" Mr. Mee's mustache wiggled. He likes to play this game he calls "Stump the Librarian" when we have library.

"How much will you pay me if I get it right?" I said.

Mr. Mee scowled.

"I need to make some money."

Mr. Mee adjusted his eyeglasses. "I shudder at the preposition I'm about to dangle," he said, "but I must ask: What does an eleven-year-old person like yourself need money for?"

"Girl stuff!" I said at the exact same time that Winky said, "Boy stuff!"

"Answer the question," said Mr. Mee.

"Mount Everest." I'd decided to answer his first question and leave the second question alone. I absolutely positively 100 percent knew it was Mt. Everest. I was counting the money in my mind already, assuming we could come to terms.

"Mauna Kea," said Mr. Mee.

"What?"

"On Hawaii. Mauna Kea is 13,799 feet above sea level, 33,465 feet from its bottom, at the ocean floor, to its summit." Mr. Mee cocked his head, maybe to fix his mind's eye on a spot somewhere in the distance, probably the summit of Mauna Kea. Maybe to think about longing and shape poems. "That's fully three quarters of a mile taller than Mount Everest," he said.

"Try me again," I said. "And I really need to

make some sufficient funds, here." Winky's and my ideas hadn't earned squat.

"What is the world's largest living thing, and no, I am not going to pay for your answer."

"A whale!" I said. "A blue whale."

"A sperm whale!" shouted Bubba from over in the Juvenile Humor section.

"The largest living thing in the world is . . . a mushroom," said Mr. Mee.

Ripley's Believe It or Not! had failed me.

"The fungus is located in the Malheur National Forest, in the state of Oregon. The beast covers more than two thousand acres, mostly underground, all connected. Some say it's as much as eight thousand years old."

"I don't even care about that one," I said, although it *was* interesting.

"What were Cinderella's slippers made from?" asked Mr. Mee.

Even when I was saying "glass," anybody could tell by Mr. Mee's evil grin that even this, a *known fact of childhood*, was about to get ruined.

"Squirrel fur."

"Oh, brother."

"That's right," said Mr. Mee. "Charles Perrault misheard the word *vair*, meaning squirrel fur, in the oral tale he recorded and updated, for the similar-sounding *verre*, or glass. Who invented baseball?"

One thing about Mr. Mee, he isn't one to gloat. He barrels straight on to the next thing.

Winky started to speak, but I shushed him up by being louder and faster. "Abner Doubleday!"

"Wrong again. It was someone in England."

"Someone Who? Who Someone?" Winky asked.

"I'm sorry, I can't be more specific. But the game of baseball was first named and described in 1744 in an English volume entitled *A Little Pretty Pocket-Book*."

"That sounds like a stupid book," said Bubba Davis. For once I agreed with him.

Mr. Mee poked at his eyeglasses. "Let us remember the words of the mystic Suso, in *The Little Book of Truth*," he said.

Who was Suso? Their book at least sounded more promising than that pretty little pocket one.

"By ignorance the truth is known."

That didn't make any little bit of sense whatsoever. But old Suso gave me a great idea. In an instant I figured out how I could pay the new mortgage bill by April 15th. Mr. Mee always talks about his blessings, and I just hoped that by blessings he meant financial. I jabbed Winky to mean: listen to this!

"I'll bet you I can find a fact that you don't already know, Mr. Mee. And if I do, what'll you give me?" I asked. I was already scanning the bookshelves out of the corner of my eye. There's no way Mr. Mee can have read every single word in this library, I was thinking. All I had to do was find one thing he didn't already know, and I would win the bet.

"For money?" Mr. Mee was shaking his head. "I'm not about to engage a minor in gambling."

"Not gambling, Mr. Mee. Betting! For fun! And money!"

"Certainly not. If you find a fact I don't already know, I'll gladly give you my highest compliment: a hearty handshake," he said.

"Okay, but instead of your idea about the hearty handshake," I said, "for now let's just say 'prize winnings to be determined.'"

Bubba Davis's head swiveled to Mr. Mee.

"Let's not," said Mr. Mee.

Bubba swiveled his head back my way, tennis-match style.

"I already said it." I picked up my backpack and slung it over my shoulder. "Respectfully. See you later, Mr. Mee," I said.

"What will you give me, Josie," Mr. Mee said behind me, "if you fail?"

I didn't even turn around. "Squirrel-fur slippers."

I really needed those prize winnings.

A Kind of Faith

I borrowed a bunch of big, giant reference books from homeroom, so I could win that bet. By the time I was halfway home, I was panting and sweating and my shoulders felt like somebody'd stuck a hot poker between them. So I stopped to rest at the baseball field. I dropped my backpack in the patchy grass behind the backstop and hung my fingers from the chain-link fencing. Only a week or so ago there had still been a little snow hanging around the shady edge of the baseball field, and here the team was all in shirtsleeves.

Winky was sitting on one end of the players' bench. I knew I was too far away for him to see me, but I didn't call out to him, because he was on duty. He loves baseball so much, he'd settled for being the team's water boy.

"Maximal torque!" Coach Clay was shouting to the players on the infield. "Elbow position . . . think about where your power comes from . . ."

Winky tidied a small stack of towels. Then he lined up a couple of water bottles.

"Your head and shoulders, now, you want to keep some distance between 'em . . . ," Coach Clay said to a player.

Winky walked over to the fenced enclosure at the side of the field where a wheel pitching machine was set up, and he turned it on. Then he got in front of the machine and took up position.

Uh-oh.

I have tried to squint and blur my vision and imagine what it would be like to have such terrible eyesight as Wink's. "Winky," I asked him one time, "if you wanted to describe how it is you see things, would you say it was a color?"

"Maybe. Yeah, maybe a color." Winky thought a minute. "Green," he said. "Spotty green."

"If it's green, would you call it lime green, or grass green, or some other kind of green?"

"Green with black in it."

"Green with black in it is . . . Winky, they don't make that color. That seems like it would just be black. The black would cancel out the green."

"Okay, maybe green with a lightning storm in it. At midnight."

"The storm is at midnight."

"Right. In a hot place like Florida that's also freezing cold."

This is why it surprised me that Winky was squaring off with a ball machine, and—

Crack!—and why I was surprised when he hit it! The ball went straight and low and caught in the netting beyond.

Again a ball came out of the wheels and— *Crack!*—he hit it.

"It's a dance of balance and stride . . . ," the coach was saying now to the players.

Crack!

"Short quick swing . . ."

Crack!

"You want that ball to jump off the bat . . ."

Crack! I could hardly believe my eyes. Wink was hitting every ball.

Crack!

"Listen, Fiske, you wanna—"

Crack!

Coach Clay turned and watched Winky swing and connect.

Crack!

"Coach, you were say—"

"Shhhhhh-shhh-*shush!*" Coach Clay flippered both hands in the direction of Jim Fiske without taking his eyes off Winky.

Crack!

The coach took off his cap, scratched the very top of his head with one fingertip, spat in the dirt, shoved the cap back on his head, and tugged the brim.

Crack!

"Hey, Water Boy!" Coach yelled.

Winky turned toward the coach's voice, but not before stepping out of range of the next ball.

"Get your buttinsky over here!" hollered Coach Clay. Winky shut the machine down, then walked toward the infield. The boys watched. I moved from where I stood behind home base over to the bleachers to keep out of the way.

"What're you doing over there, Elwyn?"

"Nothing much," said Winky. He poked himself between the eyes to push up his dark sunglasses.

Nothing much! I thought. You just hit every single ball that came firing out of that machine

top-speed! *And you're legally blind!* Which is basically what Coach Clay said. He removed his cap
again, scratched, spat, replaced the cap. He rubbed
his jaw and squinted. Winky stood there while
Coach Clay ran through his routine.

"How do you do it?" Coach finally sputtered like
a cartoon character. "You can't even see the ball!"

The boys mumbled.

"Good question, Coach," Winky began. "I can't
see the ball very well—it's sort of a fuzzy place in
the sides of my vision." He shrugged. "I just know
the ball is on its way, and I just know where it's
going to show up over the plate and when it's going
to get there."

The coach looked Winky up and down like
he was Coach Monkey and Winky was a bunch of
bananas. "Whaddaya say you hit what I throw ya,
Elwyn. Ya think you can do that?"

"Naw," said Winky.

Coach Clay ignored him. "Man versus machine
is one thing, but mano a mano is another slice of
pepperoni," he said. "Tell you what. I'll shovel as
many snowballs as you can hit, okay?"

"Okay, Coach," said Winky. Like I said, he's a
try-er.

Winky went and stood at the plate.

"Here we go, nice and easy." Coach wound up

and pitched one slow and in the strike zone.

Winky made contact.

"Attaboy!"

Winky grinned.

Then Coach Clay unleashed his inner All-Star.

I'd like very much to say that Winky hit them all. He did not. Hit any.

"All right, that's enough," Coach Clay said at last. He stuffed his glove under his armpit and rubbed his elbow. Some of the players began to grumble.

The Coach walked to the plate and Wink held the bat as if he didn't know what to do with it. "Oh, well. Worth a try, son. You mighta been a miracle."

Winky shrugged again. "I used to hit 'em all, when I could still see. I was a very promising Pee Wee player."

Some of the boys snickered at *Pee Wee*.

Coach Clay ran a hairy hand over his stubbly chin. "Well, you sure can hit 'em outta the Iron Mike. I'll give you that."

Coach Clay put his hand on Winky's back and turned him to face the team. It was just the two of them out in front of all the other boys. He squeezed Winky's shoulder and didn't let go. Everything was very quiet while Coach Clay chewed on his lip and looked at his own feet. Then he looked at the boys and said, in a thin sort of voice that sounded like he needed to have a good hard swallow, "This here's a kid who'd give anything to be able to play the beautiful game you ay-hats take for granted."

So maybe it wasn't the big league. But to hit like that? To stand there and swing away again and again, when he can't even see the ball coming at him? I admire Winky Wheaton for that. I would say it shows a kind of faith. The shape of Winky's longing would be a bat.

Knock-Knock

I headed straight home from the field. But as I came down the driveway, the Way was Not Open. There were seven or eight of them, squirrels, all wicked busy leaping and springing on the steps leading up to the mudroom off the kitchen. Seven or eight isn't a big number when you're talking toes, or twenty-point pop-quizzes, or M&Ms, but it is when it's squirrels. They—all of them—stopped and looked at me. Wicked creepy. Was it my imagination, or did those squirrels lean toward me *all as one*, like a giant Oregon fungus?

I stood verrrrry still. Just then Grandpa's bald head came into view through the window. He waved. I went "Squir-rels!" without making a sound. I didn't want the squirrels to know I was onto them. Grandpa opened the window. The squirrels startled, but only for a second. Then out came sailing a handful of peanuts in the shell. The squirrels went wild. I saw my chance and dashed by them up the stairs and into the house.

"You scared them," Grandpa said.

"They scared me," I said. "You hate squirrels, Grandpa."

"I admire their industry."

"You worry they'll nest in the attic."

He looked out the window and rubbed his chin, probably thinking about the nesting and the attic.

"I bet I could train them," he said.

After a snack (I went for the peanuts, but Grandpa swatted my hand away. "They're for the squirrels!") and a little math homework, and a one-dish supper of Bush's baked beans (two cans for a dollar) with Starpact tuna fish (79 cents) and salsa (splurge), and cleaning up the kitchen (easy—two bowls, two spoons, two cups), I went up to my room to gain knowledge. I know I fell asleep at some point, because I was suddenly *not* asleep.

My bedside table lamp was still on. *Ripley's You Will NOT Believe It!* was open on my stomach.

Mom's old teddy bear, Toddles, lay very still beside me. I replayed the last few seconds in my head, and heard in my mind's ear what had woken me: the cough of Grandpa's truck starting up.

I fell asleep again listening for the sound of its return.

I dreamed about Amanda Mandolin. In the dream, Mandy Mandolin was running after a speeding truck. It was a big yellow truck. For some reason, the truck had no brakes. There was one of those runaway truck ramps you see on the highway up through Pinkham Notch. I could see the truck ramp, the way it went practically straight up, and then it would go all into shards of a picture. Then I could see it again, in and out of focus like that. The seeing clearly and not-seeing the truck ramp went on for a while, or maybe it was only a short while; you never can tell, in dreams. Then Mandy caught up to the runaway truck and jumped up onto the step thingy, reached in the driver's side window and cranked the wheel hard to get it to go up the truck ramp and stop. There wasn't any driver. But the passenger side fit three people—Mom, Grandpa, Winky. This time, though, Mandy couldn't save the day. She couldn't turn the wheel in time. The truck kept speeding and speeding away. And then it was *me* on the step thingy, trying to crank the steering wheel. And a voice yelled, "9-1-1, jump off, jump off!" I jumped. And then I was standing beside Amanda Mandolin. The truck went speeding, speeding away. The two of us had to watch it go.

"What will happen?" I said to Mandy Mandolin. And Mandy Mandolin said, "I surely do not know. But I have faith in things seen fuzzily."

I thought about that, later, when I woke up and wasn't dreaming anymore. It was confusing. Dreams are like that.

In the morning, Grandpa was whistling like he hadn't got one single care in the world. I asked him where he'd gone last night.

"Nowhere."

"Well, somebody must have taken your truck because I heard it. Maybe the squirrels. Did you train a crack team of squirrels to drive a stick shift?"

Grandpa made a big deal of pulling a handkerchief from his pocket and blowing his nose.

"Maxwell House!" he blurted.

"You left the house late at night to buy Maxwell House coffee?"

"Mm-*hmm*! The Pay 'n Takit. They're open till ten."

I looked in the blue can of coffee on the counter, the same can of ground coffee he'd scooped from yesterday, and it was half-full. It was definitely not a new can bought at ten o'clock last night!

"It looks like there was plenty of Maxwell House, Grandpa," I said.

Grandpa's mouth shifted around like he was worrying a wad of bubble gum. He folded up the *Hamburg Catch-up!*, including the funnies. Then he stood up and looked straight at me with eyes as sharp as laser beams.

"Knock-knock," Grandpa said.

So *I* said, "Who's there?"

"Money."

"Money who?"

"Money'd your own business."

While I sat there with my mouth hanging open, Grandpa shoved the newspaper under his arm, made a tight turn, and marched out of the kitchen.

Now Grandpa's fibbing, I thought. He was a fibber. They say it takes one to know one.

Graphs

On Monday I called an emergency breakfast meeting with Winky. I told him all about what happened, including the knock-knock joke, which he agreed was pretty good.

"And that's not all." I looked over one shoulder and then the other, in case of intruders like Mrs. Blyth-Barrow or Becky Schenck. "Later, when I went to pay the electric bill, I saw in the checkbook register that we were *all caught up*. He had already paid the bills and the mortgage for the month. So does that mean everything's okay, you think? Does that mean I don't have to worry anymore?"

Winky slowly chewed his French Toast Fingers. "It's mysterious," he said. "Money comes in, money goes out, and you keep your fingers crossed."

"Right. That's good," I said. "I should burn that onto a wood plaque."

Over the next couple weeks, I noticed a sort of pattern to the money coming in and going out. Grandpa would go out in the night, and the next day or two I might find cash hidden in the usual odd places in the house. Or there would be more money in the bank account according to the checkbook ledger, or I would put the money into the bank account. Grandpa might be sucking on a lollipop, and so I knew he'd been to the Anchor Bank. Sometimes, though, after Grandpa went out in the night or at other times of day, if I dropped by the Anchor Bank to see nice Mrs. Gagne, I'd find there was *less* money in the bank account. And there was always the obvious question of whether or not I was seeing all the bills. Also, whether I was aware of when Grandpa went out in the night. Sometimes I do sleep very soundly.

Meanwhile, Winky and I had several good money-maker ideas:

We set up for a carwash, but it snowed three inches (!) and nobody came.

We planned a talent show, but nobody who had any talent would agree to let us keep the proceeds.

We pulled together a bake sale, outside the

Pay 'n Takit. Mr. Miller let us borrow a card table from his storeroom, the same table the Jubilation Girls use every August to sell their famous rock-candy necklaces and bracelets. Jewelry you can eat! Genius.

"What's the bake sale for?" asked a friendly woman, eyeing my Betty's Better Butter mix brownies and snapping open her purse.

"To make money," I said.

"For what?"

"For me."

Winky smacked his forehead.

That lady wasn't the only one who didn't care to buy baked goods that weren't for the school, or the mothers, or the team, or the firefighters. We did not enjoy the same sweet success as the Jubilation Girls.

All the while, I kept a stash of cash in the Keds box under my bed. Everyone knows it's important to save for a rainy day. Even when you have a long string of rainy days, there could always be a day that's even rainy-er.

In math class, we did a unit on graphs. They always tell you math applies to real life, and here was a chance to make me believe it! If I could make a "diagrammatical illustration" of my "set of data,"

I could use it to make "educated decisions."

Wicked! That's just what I needed!

I drew a graph where one line was *M* for Money and the other line was *G* for Grandpa's Whereabouts. It ended up looking like a very poorly planned city skyline, where some of the skyscrapers actually went under the ground.

"I don't understand this graph," said Mrs. Blyth-Barrow.

"Me neither!" I said.

"How do *M* and *G* relate?"

"Exactly!" I said.

"This graph makes no sense, Josie."

"Don't I know it!" I said.

Mrs. Blyth-Barrow was not impressed, and neither was I. Once again, math was useless in real life.

I failed the assignment.

Laundry

That's not all I failed.

I missed a bill. A big bill. The same bill a couple of times, I guess.

Which is why I was doing emergency laundry in the girls' bathroom at school.

"Hey, Brillo."

Great. Becky Schenck.

"Are you doing what I think you're doing?"

"What do you think I'm doing?"

"Washing socks and underwear in the girls' bathroom."

I wasn't about to tell Becky Schenck I'd missed the water bills and the water was shut off at home.

I squeezed out my clothes and rolled them up in a long length of paper towels.

"You have zero imagination, Becky," I said, and walked out the door.

This was officially an emergency of life.

Mr. Mee's Weak Spot

Forget about car washes and bake sales. My money was on Mr. Mee.

I was still trying to win my bet (prize winnings to be determined) with Mr. Mee, and counting on him being rich. I'd pretty much exhausted my supply of *Ripley's Believe It or Not!* facts, but that was okay, because at the public library I'd found a book just loaded with this stuff.

"I've got one you won't know," I said when I stopped in the school library after school. I crossed my fingers for luck. "Answer me this: What is the driest place on earth?"

I knew he'd say Sahara Desert. I hoped he'd say

Sahara Desert. Who wouldn't say Sahara Desert?

Mr. Mee didn't say Sahara Desert. He said, "Antarctica."

"Oh, forget it," I said. I leaned over, yanked *The Book of General Ignorance* out of my backpack, and put it on the counter. It made a thud. The amount of general ignorance, page-wise, is vast. Even Suso would be impressed.

Mr. Mee eyed the book. "An excellent resource."

"You've read it?"

"Of course," said Mr. Mee. "I read everything."

"You know a lot," I said to Mr. Mee, "even for a librarian."

Mr. Mee kind of snorted. "Thank you," he said. Then he picked up his bottle of water and held it in front of me. "But that's a bit like saying I'm in possession of a lot of water. When you consider the incalculable amount of H_2O there is on the planet, I'm nearly waterless." He wiggled the water bottle and it sloshed. "There are puddles and ponds and lakes and lochs, oceans and rivers of knowledge whose existence we have never even guessed at, let alone explored in our leaking, bobbing boats."

"If you say so," I said. I hoisted my backpack onto my shoulder.

"Josephine," Mr. Mee began, "I meant what I said."

"When you said what." My backpack slid down my arm and I hitched it up again.

"I'm much older than you are," said Mr. Mee. "I've read more. But in the great scheme of life, I don't know any more than you do. And you know things about which I know nothing." He smiled and adjusted his glasses. "I've merely the one bottle of water."

"Hey!" I said. "That reminds me. Did you know you can drown in a teacup?"

"Yes."

"Rats."

Mr. Mee pointed at me. "You have a water bottle too. And in time, you'll see that all the water you really need is already in the bottle."

I guessed I'd have to think on that, along with the words of Suso.

That's when Winky Wheaton stumbled in, wearing his baseball cap and carrying an armload of the large-print books Mr. Mee orders for him, which was only four, each one being practically as large as *The Book of General Ignorance*.

"On your way to baseball practice, Elwyn?" said Mr. Mee.

"Yup," said Winky.

"That's the one with the net and the putter and the whiffles, yes?" he said. A joke.

"And the kilts," said Winky Wheaton, playing along.

Aha and aha! I thought, willing my face not to do anything lively. Three can play *that* game. The game of sports. Mr. Mee does not know anything about sports! I'd found Mr. Mee's one weakness.

Sneakily, I waited till Mr. Mee was busy in the reference stacks and the parent volunteer had taken over the desk. Then I checked out all the sports books I could fit in my backpack. *The Psychology of Champions, Principles and Practice of Sports Management,* and *Soccernomics,* to name a few of the titles. I also borrowed a two-inch stack of *Sports Unlimited* back issues, and some recent newspapers, for the Sports section. Then I put on the blank expression I perfected in coed health class, and walked right by Mr. Mee and out the door.

Becky Gets Creative

Turns out I was wrong about Becky having no imagination. She hung a long chain of crafty cut paper all around my desk and chair, only instead of a string of paper dolls holding hands in the spirit of friendship, it was underwear on a clothesline. Very funny, Becky.

"What is the meaning of this?" Mrs. Blyth-Barrow wanted to know.

"Ask Josie!" said Becky Schenck.

I crumpled up the whole string of Becky's little art project and shoved the wad of construction paper out of sight in my desk.

Becky answered for me. "She peed her pants!

She was washing them in the bathroom! That's against the rules!"

"Josie, please see me in the hall."

"Me? What about her?" I said.

I could hear a long *pssssssss* behind me as I followed Mrs. B-B out of the classroom.

"What's going on, Josie?" Mrs. B-B's voice was soft and gentle as a "Peace be with you" at church. I almost told her the truth. But Becky making fun of me wasn't the problem. Mrs. B-B finding out about Grandpa and the bills was the problem.

"I did that, what Becky said," I told her. "I—I had an accident."

Mrs. B-B looked thoughtful, is how I'd put it. "Is there anything you need, Josie?" she said. "Anything at all?"

Sometimes when people are nice to you, you're afraid you'll crack and all the goo—feelings and sadness and all that—will leak right out. You're afraid there won't be any going back. So I said, "No! Nothing!" as if *she* was the crazy one.

A Sour Note

Joe Viola got sent down!" cried Winky Wheaton. He waved a newspaper right in my face. His magnifying glass jumped on its lanyard.

Grandpa must have paid the water bill somehow, and I hadn't had to wash any more clothes in the girls' bathroom, so that was good. Also good: the cafeteria was serving Oaty Cakes for breakfast. I dug in. "Shent dow' where?" I said.

"To the Hot Dogs, of course! Don't you know anything?" he added, wicked happy. I don't know if I'd ever seen all his teeth at once like that.

"But this can't mean anything good about his sluh—hah, hmm, his you know what."

"I know and yes it's bad news for the Believers' shot at the playoffs, that's for sure, but still I can't

believe it. I get to meet him in person! I don't even
have to go to Boston, where my parents won't let me
even go anyhow, and it's just till he gets his game
back, it's not like he'll be here long, but he's been
tanking in Boston and oh this is exciting! Must.
Remain. Calm." Winky was breathing shallow and
talking wicked fast.

I grabbed the newspaper. VIOLA HITS SOUR
NOTE. "Catchy!" I said.

Winky: *glare, glare, glare.*

Me: "A viola is a musical instrument?"

Winky: "I KNOW THAT!"

Well, I still say the *Hamburg Catch-up!* has a
way with words.

Winky grabbed the paper back and pressed it
to his chest and squeezed out a noise I'd never heard
before and hoped I'd never hear again. Kids as far
away as the table by the emergency exit turned and
stared.

That reminded me of the time I asked Winky, "How
about if you wanted to describe how you see as a
sound, could you do it that way?"

Winky: "Yes. It's definitely a high, static sound,
like a piercing, almost silent scream of a lady
dressed all in white. And with long, white-white,
super-white hair."

Me:

Winky: "And at the same time it's low, very low, a vibration really, like an earthquake, it's so low."

Me:

Winky: *shrug.*

Me: "So it's a high and low sound, both, plus shaking."

Winky: "Right."

Me:

The closest Winky could ever get to some description I could use to understand his vision was "kaleidoscopic in the center, with a ring of reality around the edges." No Major League Baseball player sees that ball coming toward his bat through a kaleidoscope and hits it. No way, no how. But Winky could.

I poked the newspaper. "Well, bad news for Joe Viola is good news for us!" I said.

And Winky said, "*Eeeeeeee!*"

One Prong Short

The sun was low by the time Grandpa's truck rolled down the driveway after a couple hours on Saturday running errands. We sat there and remained silent, like the plaque tells us to, while the truck coughed and lurched and stopped. I checked out the truck window to count the number of squirrels compared to me. (Math!) At first it had been just a couple of squirrels. Grandpa liked putting some peanuts-in-the-shell on the mudroom steps, and watching the squirrels come and get them and hide them away. By then we were outnumbered like the last of the living in a zombie movie and going through a bag of nuts a day.

Grandpa went out to his workshop in the garage, and I went in and made the macaroni. When I called, "Dinner!" Grandpa came inside carrying a little wooden house. It had a pointy little flagpole on its little tiny porch, and a hole where a front door would be. "It's a squirrel house," he told me. "I'll shove an ear of corn on this spike, and Mister Nutkin can sit right here and nibble away. And he can go inside for a snooze, if he likes."

We ate dinner with the squirrel house in the middle of the table, right beside the ketchup. Grandpa kept moving it a little this way or that way, sliding it a half inch to the left, pushing one corner to get a better view.

"Do you want a salad? Is it salad you want?" I said. I was thinking about that full-color brochure and the salad bar at the old folks' home.

"Sure, sure," Grandpa said.

"We could make vegetables some nights."

"Right you are," he said.

We ate our macaroni in silence for bit.

"Rutabaga!" said Grandpa.

"It's nice, Grandpa," I said. I meant the squirrel house.

Grandpa smiled proudly, as if he'd built the Great Pyramid of Giza. "This squirrel house is going to make us a lot of money, Josie."

"It is?" Money! Yay!

"See, I'm not going to make just the one," he said. "This is what we call a prototype. I'll make a *hundred* squirrel houses."

A hundred squirrel houses?

"And sell 'em," said Grandpa. He tapped the side of his nose and narrowed his eyes.

Do people really want to invite a lot of squirrels to their yards? is what I was wondering, when Grandpa pushed his chair back and got up. "Thanks for the chow," he said. "Places to go, people to see. Man of action! Not a thing in the world to worry about." Then he dashed out the door and to the truck to go who knows where, trailing squirrels as he went.

"If it wasn't for the squirrels, I might have believed him," I said to Winky. We were swinging on the tire swing at Winky's house. We could hear the TV going full blast inside, through the window. I wound myself up and stuck out my feet and let the tire spin. "You should get Joe Viola to show up," I said. Winky's idol had been in town a whole week already, and Winky still hadn't gone to try to meet him. Winky said he "oughta get a haircut first," "had to clean the garage," and was "coming down with something."

"You said he's a charity machine," I said. I spun a little. "I'm a charity."

Winky went inside and came back out with a snack of leftover Super Tuna Noodle-Bake and two forks. We ate to the tune of the opening music of *The Sands of Time*.

"Fingers crossed isn't going to cut it," I said to Winky. Then I laid out my three-pronged plan for keeping Grandpa and me afloat:

Schemes, like the carnival and the yard work.

Grandpa's mystery money: cash, deposits, withdrawals.

My bet with Mr. Mee.

Winky climbed onto the tire swing and kicked it around. "This plan is one prong short of a typical fork," he said.

Then I heard something that gave me a big idea. It was characters talking on the TV. "You're dead to me, Brock!"

I thought about that. I thought of Mom's explanation of my dad. "Dead to me!" But not *actually* dead. No more dead than Brock was, probably.

I grabbed Winky's feet when they spun by and stopped the tire in its tracks. "I know what the fourth prong is."

A Memory at Moody's

G randpa, are you sure, a hundred percent, that you don't know anything about my dad?"

I had gone up to the attic to search for clues to the fourth prong. Before then, I had never been tall enough to reach the string for the pull-down stairs! Up there with the spiderwebs, I'd found a commemorative keepsake birth certificate with my name and two tiny inky footprints and a tiny pink bow; some old Boston Believers programs; ticket stubs to various events; some old clothes; some snapshots of people I didn't know. Was one of the men in the pictures my father? Grandpa didn't know who anybody was.

Now we were at Moody's for breakfast, sitting in our favorite booth. I'd heard the truck go out again in the night, and in the morning Grandpa was in what he calls "fine spirits." So far, he hadn't blurted once!

"I don't know the first thing about him, Jo-Jo. She didn't like to tell me things," he said. "Your mom and I, we disagreed."

"About what?"

"Everything. Loudly. She did not enjoy having old farts for parents, for one thing. Your grandma Kaye and I had given up hope of ever having a child of our own, at our advanced age. Cindy hated our music, hated our food, why she even hated our sense of fashion." Grandpa smoothed his shirt-front, an old plaid flannel number from G-mart, and winked.

"You look good," I said.

"Thank you," he said, and took another sip of his coffee. "She never thought much of Hamburg, Maine. She left a note and hopped a bus for parts unknown the very day she graduated high school. I guess she didn't find what she was looking for, because two months later she was back. Married, divorced, and pregnant. And she settled down right here."

Disappointing. But at least we could enjoy Debbie Moody-Cote's waffles. Then, who should come bustling over but Mrs. Beverly Moody, out from under her retirement, I guess. She told us Debbie and her husband, Lewis Cote, had gone up north on vacation to Canada, and so she was minding the fort till next Thursday.

"You are well, Martin?" she said to Grandpa. Mrs. Moody's family come from Montreal, and she has that French Canadian way of talking where the words in a sentence are just a little out of order.

"Fit as a . . ." Grandpa's voice trailed off and his eyes searched the ceiling for the word, which I said.

"Fiddle."

"Fiddle!" he blurted as if he'd said it first. "Fiddle-faddle." This he added for no good reason that I could tell.

"Interested in purchasing a squirrel house, Bev?" Grandpa asked Mrs. Moody, straight out of the blue.

Mrs. Moody didn't even blink. "*Non,*" she said. She shook her head so sharp the pencil in her bun about fell out.

"Give it some thought," Grandpa said. I didn't think she would.

"Very good," said Mrs. Moody. "So." She took a little pad out of her apron pocket and the pencil from her bun. "Anything you like, you order and we whip it up."

"Pancakes!" Grandpa said.

Mrs. Moody nodded and jotted on the pad and said, "*Oui, crepes, absolument.*"

I was about to order the same thing, because everybody knows Debbie Moody-Cote just doesn't have the knack like her grandmother with those thin, delicious pancakes. But then I had a memory.

My memory was of sitting in this same booth with Mom, and how she would always order Mrs. Moody's special apple-upside-down cake. It was sticky, and cakey, and sweet and even a little bitter, which you'd think would not be tasty, but it was. It was so good, my mouth started watering just thinking about it. Mom would always put her fork down and pat her tummy and say she was too full to finish, and I'd get the very last bite, which everyone knows is the stickiest and very best bite of all. In my memory I even heard Mom's voice! I heard her! How she ordered the apple cake off the old menu, which was partly in French.

And so with Mom's voice whispering in my mind's ear, I said to Mrs. Moody, "Do you have the tart tarteen?"

Mrs. Moody tapped her pencil on her little pad and looked at me funny and cocked her head and said, "But of course, *oui*, if you like," and she wrote it down and away she went with our orders.

It wasn't too long before she came back with Grandpa's crepe pancakes, and my . . . bread and butter.

"Tart tarteen?" I said, looking up at Mrs. Moody. "Apple cake?"

"Ah, *oui*, I see, but you ordered the *tartine*." She pointed at the plate of bread and butter. "Bread and butter is *tartine*. The cake is *tarte tatin*." She tapped her ear. She said it like "ta-*taan*." She shook her head. "I don't have it today. Tomorrow, *oui*, yes. Today I can bring you out something . . . *beignet*? Fritter?"

It's sad and troubling when you forget important parts of your favorite memory.

The fritter was wicked good, though. I patted my tummy and said I was full and I gave the last bite to Grandpa.

Hot Dogs and Fireflies

That night, Winky and I went to watch the Hamburg Hot Dogs bark at the Manchester Pollywogs, under the lights. Some baseball teams have names that make you figure they buck or fight or that they're mighty or what-have-you. Hot Dogs bark. One time, a Hot Dog fan bit as well as barked, and he was escorted out by Security in the person of Asa Pike, who is also an officer at the county courthouse in downtown Hamburg.

It was Joe Viola's first game as a Hot Dog. "How does he look?" Winky wanted to know. "Looking fit? Looking ready? Looking hungry?" He punched his fist into his glove a couple of times.

Joe Viola was not on the lineup for tonight's

game, but he was suited up. His red hair clashed yuckily with the hot dog–colored uniforms. He wasn't wearing Number 23, of course. That was his Boston Believers number. Now he was Number 5. He looked like a smudgy version of the Number 23 baseball card I knew so well. Sort of like the time they replaced Brock, on *The Sands of Time*, with a new actor who looked a lot like the old one but *not exactly*. Viola sat on one end of the bench, apart from the other players, tight-lipped (except for when he spat a stream of brown liquid out the side of his mouth) and greasy-cheeked and unshaven and basically the Webster's dictionary picture of a slump.

"Good!" I said to Winky. "Looking good!"

I was on the edge of my seat, even though baseball is wicked boring. I was hoping to pick up some baseball fact or other that Mr. Mee didn't already know. The mascot, Harry the Hot Dog, was doing his job, waving his skinny arms at Manchester's bug-eyed Pollywog. Harry's legs stick out the bottom of the buns, so he can waddle-run around the bases before the start of every game. The puffy foam hood goes over the head of the person inside the costume, and rises up high, making the whole hot dog about seven feet tall. Harry does a push-up every time a Hot Dog player crosses home plate. He does his push-ups on a grassy spot just outside first base, so that the zigzag of yellow mustard down the front of the hot dog doesn't get too dirty. I would never ever wish legal blindness on anybody, but there are some things it's better not to see.

Winky listened to Mr. Schmottlach's play-by-play with one ear, and to the crowd and the crack of the bat with the other ear. In the middle was his face, which had a big smile on it. The two mascots led the fans in a seventh-inning stretch. When it was all over, Harry ended up having to do eight push-ups beside first base, and the Pollywog did five push-ups. Yay, Dogs!

"Well, here's your chance, Wink!" I said. "Let's go get Joe Viola's autograph."

Winky shook his head. He shook all over, actually. "Naaayalll. Naahht—noh—not guh," he said. The guy wasn't even speaking in English.

"I hear you," I said. "Next game. Give him a chance to get used to the place, right?"

"Guh."

On the dusky walk home, we passed by Weston's big blueberry field. Everything was quiet, since most of the Hot Dogs' traffic goes straight out to Route 4 and not into town. A light caught my eye in my side vision. I turned quick, but it was gone. Then a second light blinked in the corner of my other eye.

Gone! Keeping an eye on fireflies is about as easy as spotting a shooting star—there and gone, and then you wonder if you really saw it at all.

As soon as the snow melts, Hamburg is full of insects. For biters, we have black flies, horseflies, deer flies, moose flies, midges, no-seeums. And we have pinchers, of course, and large spiders (some of them colorful and striped and I am only pretending to be cool about this), and once I had to scrape a leech from my ankle after a dip in Pickerel Pond. But all of the biters and pinchers and spiders and leeches are worth it, long about the month of June.

I stopped walking and tugged on Wink's sleeve.

"Can you see them, Winky?" I said. "The fireflies?"

Winky faced into the field and stood quietly for a few moments.

"No."

"Remember when we used to run around and catch them in a Hellmann's jar?"

"No." He turned his head a little one way and then the other way, as if he was trying to hear the fireflies since he couldn't see them. Maybe he was just trying to jog his memory by moving his head side to side. "No," he said again.

"Oh." Winky forgot fireflies. Ouch, my heart! Like that horror movie I watched by accident at

Bonny Bodeau's birthday party in third grade, where an alien stuck a pointy hand straight into this lady's chest and squeezed. Bonny was my friend, but she moved away to Portland when her mom got a job there. Anyway, memories can be like that. Like aliens squeezing your heart.

"Well," I said, "they're little jabs of light. Blinky light. Flashes every which way."

I was explaining fireflies about as well as Winky explained how he sees. Some things are too *much*, too *large*, to talk about even for someone with all their senses. I closed my eyes.

"If you can imagine soft pulses of greenish light, so bright and . . . surprising . . . you figure they might sound like chimes or . . . or light sabers! Or flutes! But they're silent, like a bunny rabbit hiding. And there isn't any pattern to how they go on and off," I told him, "no human pattern anyway."

Winky didn't say anything. He didn't even have his eyes open.

I tried again. I had to! "It's like . . . fairies talking."

Still he didn't open his eyes. He just stood there. Maybe I wasn't helping him get it. Maybe I was making him feel bad. And then *I* was feeling really bad, because it was just . . . really important that Winky remember fireflies—how they blink and glow and catch you by surprise like how Mom used to put candles on cupcakes even if it wasn't my birthday and how could he forget fireflies?

Then Winky said, "I think I can hear them. The fairies talking."

I let out all the breath I didn't know I'd been holding.

Winky opened his eyes and smiled. "I have pretty good hearing," he said.

Winky walked me home from the game and continued on his way. The mudroom steps were clear. The squirrels must have been sleeping, or else watching me under cover of darkness. Because it was pretty dark. The porch light wasn't even on. I let myself in. Grandpa wasn't home. His note read "Gone fishin'," which is what he writes to let me know all is well, he'll be back soon, won't be late.

But it *was* late. He hadn't come back soon.

Grandpa?

I ran out the door and up the driveway, skittering pea gravel under my Keds, and called out into the night: "Winky!" And my friend turned around and came back. He's my *best* friend, after all.

"He's been out at night before," Winky said. "He's gone out in the *middle* of the night. How come you're worried?"

"There's a difference between sneaking out, and just—just not bothering to be home in the first place!" I said.

Winky pointed out that when Grandpa first started sneaking out at night and lying about it, it seemed really bad. And the next time it didn't

seem so bad, and then it was not normal, but normal for us.

"This is not normal!" I said. "Can you just be quiet and help me find him?" I said.

"That's what I'm doing!"

"Okay!" I was not being very friendly, and I didn't know why.

Winky patted my shoulder. "It's okay to be scared," Winky said.

"Duh, I know that!" Still not friendly.

We walked left on Maine Street past the courthouse and the bank, as far as Moody's Diner. We turned down Desirable Street and went by Unexpected House, and it looked creepy at night. We saw the TV on at Winky's, and his parents sitting on the couch. We kept going. Right on Pine past the cemetery, right on Garden Street, left and back down Maine along the other side, left on Portland Avenue, by Books 'n Things, the Pay 'n Takit. No Grandpa.

We walked on. "He's going out at night and leaving me alone. He's doing something he doesn't want me knowing about. Maybe he's unhappy." I thought about that full-color brochure in the secretary. "Maybe he's out trying to make new friends. Maybe he's trying to make *lady*-friends. Maybe he

should go to the Downeast Best Rest, where there are lots of vegetables and old ladies!"

"Holy moly, calm down! Josie! Listen." Winky stopped walking, so I did too. He put his hand on my shoulder right there in the middle of Portland Avenue and gave me a tiny little shake. "He can't move into a home."

"Why not?" I was still breathing hard.

"My great-aunt Georgia is in a home."

"So? Grandpa should join her!"

"Aunt Georgia drools. Here's a lady who always wore pearls, and a cardigan sweater buttoned to the neck. Mom got out of bed on Saturday, and put on a different tent-dress, the gray one, and she took me to see Aunt Georgia, and you want to know what she was wearing?"

"Nope! I do not!"

"A Hot Dogs sweatshirt. Hot Dogs!" he said, wicked loud, "in block letters so big I didn't need this," he said, waving his magnifier. "And embroidery of Harry the Hot Dog! It's insulting."

"So she's proud of our team. Go, team!" I crossed Pine and started walking toward Route 4. Winky caught up and tugged my arm till I stopped.

"There were sweatpantssss," he said. "Matching sweatpants." He swallowed, and his Adam's apple slid up and down. "You want to know what the

sweatpants said in big block letters?" Winky asked.

"Nope! No sir!"

"Hot-hot-hot," Winky said. "Hot-hot-hot!" he shouted, "right across the—" He shuddered. "The *bottom*," he whispered. "Aunt Georgia is ninety-four years old. They've got her on drugs or something to regulate her moods, or else she'd never be caught dead in that get-up."

I thought about Great-Aunt Georgia's buttons and pearls, and her matching sweatshirt and pants. I thought about the drugs.

"I'm telling you," Winky said. "It was sad."

I don't know anything about drugs, but I'm sure Grandpa doesn't like drugs any more than he likes to wear sloppy clothing with logos.

"And that's not the major reason your grandpa can't go and live at the Downeast Best Rest," Winky was saying. He leaned so close that he could look me in the eye. "Think about it, Josie." His magnifying glass swung on its lanyard and tapped me right in the stomach. "If your grandfather went away, then what would happen to you?"

Grandpa!

There's Grandpa's truck!" We'd walked right on Pine Street, all the way to where it fed onto Rural Route 4. Grandpa's truck was parked alongside some other cars in the lot of a cinderblock building that looked exactly like the criminal hangout in a TV cop-show. We waited for a lone car to pass going south, and then we crossed to the other side.

"There's no sign, no windows, it's nighttime, it's scary." I grabbed Winky's hand. "I'm scared."

"Me too," said Winky.

"Here goes," I said, and I opened the sheet-metal door.

Inside were some tables, and a long bar with a sign hung above it on the wall: LOYAL ORDER OF THE

CHICKADEE. The chickadee had a hooked beak and a crew-cut hairdo, and beady, beady eyes. I have never seen such a tough-looking chickadee.

A man behind the bar wearing an old Believers cap and peeling a hard-boiled egg looked up and stopped. Seven or eight men talking and playing cards at the tables turned their heads and stopped. The whole place stopped.

Except for one single person sitting on a spinny stool in the back of the room.

"Oranges!" he blurted.

Grandpa was not with any *lady*-friends, but he seemed very friendly with a slot machine. How I know it was a slot machine is because of its light-up name: *Slot Machine!* and slogans like *Win Win Win! Try Your Luck!* and *You Won't Win if You Don't Play!*

I had a lot of questions: Are slot machines legal? Is this why he wasn't paying the bills? Does this explain the wads of money hidden around the house? Was the cash I found money he'd won, or money he hadn't *lost* yet? What the heck is the Loyal Order of the Chickadee? But all I could say was, "Grandpa?"

The machine went *fwap-fwap-fwap-fwaahh*, like when a rascally cartoon character gets foiled by another cartoon character.

Grandpa did not seem glad to see me and

Winky. First his knees swiveled slowly in my direction, followed by his middle and shoulders, then his head, his eyes moving last from the slot machine as if they were stuck with Krazy Glue to the rolling reels of little fruits. I half expected his eyeballs to be spinning. Instead they were . . . blank.

Then the hard-boiled-eggs man hollered from behind the bar. "Members only!" he boomed. "And positively no minors allowed!"

Grandpa raised a hand. "It's all right, Leonard," he said.

The other men didn't seem too interested in a couple of minors showing up past bedtime. They went back to their muttering and their cards.

Then Leonard said, "I got the number for Child Protective Services right here."

I fake-laughed even though Leonard is a big, red-faced man with bulgy muscles and a thick neck and I didn't know if what he said about calling Child Protective Services was or was not a joke. Then Winky fake-laughed too, and even slapped his knee and shook his head like he could hardly believe what a jokester Leonard was. So then I said, "What a jokester!" and Winky said, "Funny, funny stuff." Leonard kept slowly wiping the bar top and bulging his muscles and looking hard at us from under his greasy baseball cap. Probably memorizing our features for the police report.

Grandpa slid off the stool with a last, longing glance at the slot machine. "Hope is the thing with feathers," he said. Another of his wood-burning projects, the motto that made about as much sense as the words of the mystic Suso.

Leonard waved his bar towel at us, and we all went out of the Loyal Order of the Chickadee and climbed onto the seat of Grandpa's truck to go home.

I thought about *the* Home. And I thought about *my* home. Only an hour ago I'd thought that my problem was squaring away enough money to pay some bills. But maybe those things were the least of my trouble. Maybe I had bigger problems than I thought. What if Leonard hadn't been joking about making that phone call? What if he was making that call right now?

Winky pressed his arm into my arm as if to say, "I'm here." I pressed back, to mean, "Thanks, Winky."

I had to keep Grandpa's situation—the slot machine, the mortgage statement PAST DUE, the *squirrels*, for Pete's sake—I had to keep it all a secret.

Joe Viola's First Game

Saturday afternoon's Hot Dogs game crept along like molasses running uphill on a cold day in March, as they say. More than a week had gone by since the night we found Grandpa at the Chickadee, a place he vaguely and uneasily explained was "a clubhouse, sorta."

The Hot Dogs were playing the Florida Flamingos. Winky shook like a leaf at the idea of being in the presence of his sports hero, who was pitching for the first time wearing Number 5. Joe Viola sauntered to the mound, chewing a big wad of gum and blowing lazy pink bubbles. Based on what they yelled, some people took Joe's bubble-activity as a slap in the face of the home team, since blowing

Bazooka-pink bubbles is what the fans who travel with the Flamingos always do.

"How's he looking?" Winky asked. I tried to read Joe Viola's face. Mostly, I read boredom. Gone was the smile from the card in the heart-shaped frame. He had shiny circles under his eyes, and they were not from a tube of eye black. He had not recently shaved. The number 5 buckled and sagged on his mostly untucked shirt. His posture was—sorry, Wink—slumped.

"He looks . . . awake in a way that he did not at the night game," I said kindly.

Viola tended to have a hard look for whoever was at bat. If I'd been the batter, I'd have run crying to the dugout, is what I mean by a hard look. Someone scary in an unwelcome dream might wear a look as hard as Joe Viola's.

Winky listened to Mr. Schmottlach call the play. He groaned and cheered along with every fully sighted fan.

Some of the fans yelled positive things and some of them yelled things that were not as positive. An old man with two long braids and a bandanna tied around his head had brought a violin, and every so often he'd drag the bow across the out-of-tune strings.

"His name's *Viola*, not *Violin*," Winky said.

"That guy is only embarrassing himself."

"How do you know it's a violin and not a viola?" I wondered.

"Oh, believe me, I know," Winky said. "That guy might as well be playing a French horn."

Deep in the third inning, the Dogs were down by two. One woman stood and yelled, "Give 'em what-for, Joe!" She was wearing very short purple shorts. Barely meeting the hem of the shorts was a long T-shirt with *Tina Taylor! Whole Lotta Love Tour* across the chest. She sat down again. She had very big hair, like a storm cloud gathering around her head. The people behind her had to lean or stretch up tall to see the action on the field. She hollered more, and louder, than anybody else in the stands. "Show 'em whatcha got, Joe!"

"Shaddup, Tina Taylor!" shouted that rude old man with the violin. The lady did look a lot like Tina Taylor, though.

All during the game, Winky practiced what he would say when he finally met the baseball star formerly known as Number 23.

"Hello, extend hand, it's not every day you get to meet your sports hero."

"That's good, Winky. That's very professional."

"My name is Elwyn Wheaton. I am your biggest fan."

"Nice. Good stuff, Winky."

Things like that. Over and over and over again.

In the fifth inning, Joe Viola threw his glove down and stood there with his hands on his hips, looking at the sky and shaking his head when an outfielder botched a catch and the Flamingo runner rounded third and pounded home. Viola looked like he wanted no part of his new team. He threw a couple wild pitches after that, but he finished up okay, and the Hot Dogs won 6–4.

Viola jogged off the mound and straight to the stands, where the Tina Taylor lady had made good time down the stands, even in her high heels.

"Joe Viola kissed Tina Taylor right on the mouth!" I said to Winky.

Winky frowned, and pulled at the rawhide strings of his glove. "Does she look worthy? Does she look nice?"

"How should I know?" I said. "You can't tell a book by its cover, Winky, even if your vision's 20/20."

"I know *that*," said Winky.

"Plus, people can cover up their real selves as easy as a Brenda's Book Cozy!"

"I'm just asking what she looks like!"

"She's wearing basically a mini-dress to a baseball game, for crying out loud. And those shorts are not the athletic type. Her shoes don't seem very sensible for a baseball game."

Then the lady smiled at Joe Viola. He smiled back. Hers was a confident, toothpaste-ad type smile. His was a goofy, loopy, dreamy cartoon-character-type smile.

Yes, she looked nice. Friendly.

Viola draped one arm around her shoulders like a wet towel. She stood a few inches taller than him, due to the fancy shoes. On his other wrist was slung his baseball glove. They walked in the opposite direction, across the field and away from the small, polite crowd that waited. (Violin-man had left, after being on the business end of a hard look himself from Asa Pike.)

"Well, I guess he doesn't want to see his fans just yet," said Winky, turning toward the break in the fence that was the exit.

I wasn't about to let Joe Viola get away. I grabbed Winky's arm.

"Come on!"

We chased Joe across the field.

"Hey!" I yelled.

He glanced back over his shoulder. Was it my imagination, or did he pick up his pace?

Winky and I kept jogging. Closer and closer we came. It was like a movie where the camera rushes up and stops short: Joe Viola turned around.

We nearly ran right into him. Up close, his red hair sprang tuftily from under his baseball cap. More hair could be seen in patches in the open neck of his uniform shirt.

Winky opened and closed his mouth a couple of times. He was standing really close and doing his heavy-blinking close-peering thing. Number 5 took a step backward.

"Joe Viola!" Winky squawked, stepping into the space Viola had just made between them. As if the guy didn't know his own name! Winky was losing it!

Slowly, slowly, Winky extended his right hand toward his sports hero's arm. His hand homed in on its target, as if Viola's elbow was a big red button that would set off a nuclear bomb we all had mixed feelings about launching from an underground silo. Then, very lightly, and with everyone watching, Winky's fingertips touched Viola's sleeve.

Ka-boom!

"That's my name, don't wear it out," Joe Viola said.

Winky pulled back his hand. "Did you get my letters?"

Letters?

"What letters?" said Viola. He glanced at his girlfriend.

"I sent letters." Winky drew his shoulders to

his ears and squinted hard. "A couple letters. Three or four. Maybe a half dozen or a dozen. Couple dozen—"

"Joey, honey," said the lady, and good thing or Winky might have counted to a hundred. "Why don't you sign the little boy's program or something." She turned to me. I could see my own face in her huge sunglasses. "Would he like that, sweetie?" Her hair really was a thing of beauty.

"Oh, my friend can speak very nicely for himself," I piped up. "Normally."

Nobody had anything to say about that, and the word "normally" was still hanging in the air like a speech bubble. "My friend, here, is probably your biggest fan," I said. "Don't you have anything to say, anything *nice* to say, about that?" I swallowed. "Sir?" I added. I didn't want to seem weird or unfriendly.

Joe Viola narrowed his eyes at me as if I seemed weird and unfriendly. So did the lady. So did Winky Wheaton, even.

"Thanks, kid," said Joe Viola. "That's nice." Glove dangling from his wrist, he yanked my program from my hand, whipped out a Sharpie pen, signed it, and handed the program to Winky. "I'm just a little tired," he said. "Adjusting to the time change, so to speak."

"Uhhnnn," Winky sort of mooed, like a

cow-zombie, staring at the still-glistening Sharpie on the program, which, since Winky was too paralyzed to use his magnifier, I read out loud: "For a true athletic supporter," followed by a scribbled signature that looked like "Vile." I'll say!

"Joseph," said the lady, looking concerned at Winky.

"What?"

She jutted her chin at Winky and cut her eyes at him two or three times. "Go on and buy them each a Sno-Cone." She smiled in a large way that showed every single one of her nice teeth, even the ones in back. Then she leaned toward Winky and spoke very slowly and loudly, with pauses between each word. "You, like, Sno-, Cones?"

I scowled on Winky's behalf, but my argument was not with Tina Taylor. And yes, we like Sno-Cones.

Joe Viola let all his air out—*pffffff*—like a bike tire valve, reached into his back pocket, and rolled his eyes as if buying a Sno-Cone for a blinking, multiple-letter-writing zombie and his friend was the stupidest thing he'd ever heard of. And that just made me mad. A true sports hero would buy his biggest fan a Sno-Cone without his girlfriend having to force him into being nice. I couldn't help it. I stuck my tongue out at him. I curled it for good measure, because I can do that and I figured it would look extra sassy.

He stuck his tongue out back! Wicked immature! He even curled his, too! I was right about the extra sass.

He and I stared at each other.

"Sorry, all I got's large bills," he said finally, and shrugged.

"That's okay," I said to Joe Viola's wallet. I put my hand out flat, and Viola hesitated.

All in one smooth motion, Joe Viola's girlfriend looked straight at Number 5, crossed arms over chest, tilted ear to shoulder, and popped a hip like a long-legged doll. Joe Viola watched her do this thing, and then he glared at me with the force of a hundred suns.

For a second I thought about grabbing the wallet and sprinting away with all his large bills.

Joe Viola's cheek bulged where either he shifted his chewing gum or a weird vein was pulsing. "Fine," he said, smacking a twenty onto my palm. He snapped his wallet shut and shoved it in his pocket, and as he did, his glove slipped from his wrist.

It fell

onto

the ground.

So I picked it up.

The sound of three people gasping at once is a lot louder and hissier than you might imagine.

Joe Viola clutched his chest and made a couple damp, gakking sounds, and Winky uttered two words: "Josephine Bloom!" It seemed like all Winky could do was say people's names.

"You look like you might be having a heart attack or something," I said to Joe Viola. "Are you okay?"

Viola stared at me. It wasn't the hard look he had for batters, it was more of a horrified, bug-eyed look. He took in a shuddering breath. "Am I *okay*?"

"You seem sort of—"

"Am *I* okay?"

"I mean you look a little sweaty—"

"*Am* I okay?"

"That's what I'm *asking*! That's what *I'm* asking!"

Joe Viola took the glove from my hand and whispered, "Time will tell," creepy, like he was wrapping up a ghost story around the campfire. "Only time will tell."

Joe Viola walked away. His girlfriend glanced back at me over her shoulder once, then tipped her head to his, a puffy silvery cloud above his head, and wrapped both arms around his waist, all without tripping. Those two would probably be winners at a three-legged race.

"What was *that* all about?" I said to Winky.

Winky was white as a sheet. He was opening and closing his mouth, but he still hadn't said another word. We watched his hero walk away across the field.

"You never," he finally managed to croak. "Ever," he added. "Touchabaseballplayer'sstuff!"

"Why not?"

"You could throw him in a"—his voice dropped to a whisper—"S-L-U—"

"He's already *in* a slump!"

Winky plugged his ears.

I flapped Joe Viola's twenty in Winky's face till he dropped his hands by his sides.

"Sno-Cone?" I said.

I Win the Bet with Mr. Mee

You never talk about a no-hitter or a perfect game while the game is in progress.

Don't ask a baseball player about his family.

A player won't ever put a hat on a bed.

Never ask a baseball player to spit out his gum.

Winky gave me a crash course in baseball superstitions, and I promised to study my notes even though that sounded a lot like school.

Speaking of school, soon it was the last day of it.

"Nobody is leaving until this room is spotless!" said Mrs. Blyth-Barrow.

"Smell ya later, Brillo!" said Becky Schenck. I ignored her and practically galloped home.

I got myself an after-last-day-of-school snack,

and sat down to flip through an issue of *All-Time All-Sports* magazine. My stack of sports books hadn't turned up a single thing I could say I knew that Mr. Mee didn't. I wasn't feeling as happy as usual on the last day of school because of, you know, all the problems.

I began to think I really should have run off with Joe Viola's wallet, the jerk, when I came upon something that made me sit up so fast and so straight that the bowl tipped from my lap, and mini-pretzels scattered all over the place. But who cares about the mini-pretzels? Who cares if maybe I had a rich father I had no idea how to find? Who cares about the slot machines and the bills? I could not believe my eyes! This was the best fact I'd ever come across, and I didn't care if Mr. Mee *did* already know it!

I rolled up the issue of *All-Time All-Sports* and took off running back to school in hopes a librarian's work is never done.

It isn't.

There he was.

"Mr. Mee! Mr. Mee!"

Mr. Mee put down the pen he was holding, sprang from his seat, and poked his eyeglasses.

"Believe it or not, Mr. Mee!" I flattened out

All-Time All-Sports and flipped to page 67.

Mr. Mee was quiet. Then he smiled and reached out his hand, and (heartily) I shook it.

"Now, about those prize winnings," I said.

I found Winky at the ball field. I waited while he used his ever-ready magnifier to read page 67 of *All-Time All-Sports*—which Mr. Mee himself had ripped (he used a ruler, wicked neat) right out of the magazine. I watched him as he read about the noises and the rules and the schedule, the blind-folds and the specially made ball.

"That oughta cheer you up!" I said when he looked up and let the magnifying glass drop to his chest.

Winky stared at me.

"I mean after the thing with Joe Viola."

He blinked a whole lot.

"Does it?" I asked. "Cheer . . . you up?"

Winky stood there counting to ten or something. Then he threw his arms around me, pinning mine to my sides. Then he released me. "Come on!" he said.

We followed the shortcut through the pines and got to Winky's house in no time flat. I took the porch steps in one stride and got whacked in the head by one of Mr. Wheaton's pull-up rings, which hang on blue webbing straps from overhead hooks. Mr. Wheaton is something of a fitness fanatic. Winky got the key from where it's always stashed under the mat, and stuck it in the lock. Wink's parents keep the house locked even though they are almost always at home. "In case they come looking for me," is what Mr. Wheaton says about that.

As usual, Wink's dad was sprawled on the couch, the TV on full blast. Mr. Wheaton sported a muscle-shirt on which was printed I FLEXED AND THE SLEEVES FELL OFF. The message was distended partly by comic design and partly by the fabric being stretched to its limit across Mr. Wheaton's perfectly round stomach and leaving bare the shady underbelly like an unwholesome Winnie the Pooh. (I said he was *some*thing of a fitness fanatic.) Through the open door to the back room, Mrs. Wheaton could be seen sitting up in bed, wearing a flowered housecoat and sewing on a book cozy.

Both the parents froze, as if startled to see children in their house.

"But I love you, Brock!" said a breathy voice out of the TV.

"Turn it off!" Winky said. "Quit stitching!"

I'm telling you, I was surprised by his teacher-like tone. And so must his parents have been because they did what they were told.

"What is it?" said Mr. Wheaton, thudding his stocking feet to the floor and aiming the TV clicker so enthusiastically that the tattooed hula dancer on his bicep wiggled her grass skirt. Meanwhile, Mrs. Wheaton shoved her rolling table aside, casters squealing, and rose from her bed to reveal—like the time-lapse photograph of the Amazon Rainforest we saw in science class—the full length and width of her flowered housecoat.

"I have an announcement," said Winky.

"Yeah," I said.

"There's such thing as the National Beep Baseball League, and I want to join."

Mr. Wheaton craned his neck over the back of the couch to throw a look at Mrs. Wheaton.

"Well, isn't *that* a thing!" Mrs. Wheaton said as she made her way to the couch.

Mr. Wheaton turned back around. "What the beep is that? Heh-heh," he said.

"It's a blind baseball league," Winky said.

"Blind baseball league, eh?" Mr. Wheaton scratched his underarm. "It sounds expensive."

Mrs. Wheaton wheezed and plopped down on the couch beside Mr. Wheaton. He put a hairy arm around her. The hula dancer looked uncomfortable.

"There's a team in Boston," said Winky.

Mr. Wheaton took a hard candy from the dish on the coffee table and popped it into his mouth. He squinted one eye and made an O with his lips. The candies were clearly sour balls. "You know Bosh-ton'sh a good fwee-hour drive, Elwyn," he said, speaking around the sour ball, "and that'sh not accounting for traffic."

"And the tolls!" Mrs. Wheaton remarked.

"Highway robbery!" said Mr. Wheaton.

"I could take the Peter Pan bus straight there," Wink said.

"Now, now, Elwyn, the bus costs a pretty penny too, and peopled with strangers and who knows who, murderers and felons, probly, and rough sorts like them. The Peter Pan bus is no way to travel."

Mrs. Wheaton patted her husband's arm. "It sure is not, Bob. No 'bout a doubt it. Hand me one of them candies, a yellow one. (He did.) Boston is *out* of the *question*, if anybody's askin'. But tell us more about the sports up there anyways," she said, sucking on the sour ball and beaming at Wink.

Winky pulled the article from his back pocket and handed it to me.

"You read it," he said.

I read to them about the brand-new National Beep Baseball League. I read to them about how the league has no age or gender restrictions, about how the ball's the size of a softball and how it beeps, how the bases buzz and they're blue and five feet tall. I told them about the coaching, the competition, the playoffs, the costs.

"And best of all, it says there's an invitational tournament coming up, called the Boston Beep Ball Bash. It's at Fenway High School on June twenty-fifth." I folded up the article. "And Winky should go," I said. I smiled at Mr. Wheaton. I smiled at Mrs. Wheaton. They smiled back. I thought we were all together feeling happy. Winky had lost something, something wicked important, and with it what he loved best in the world, and here I'd come upon a way for him to get it back. Not his eyesight, of course, I'm not Jesus or even a doctor, but the game he loved to play, the thing that made him feel most happy. I was feeling pretty pleased with myself.

"It sounds like a hoot, and if it were not out of the question, we'd be tickled to pieces for you to be able to go, Elwyn, and meet some other people like yourself."

At this, Winky lit right up.

"Who knew there were so many blind-as-*bats* baseball yahoos?" said Mr. Wheaton.

"Enthusiasts," said Mrs. Wheaton.

"Nuts," said Mr. Wheaton.

"Players!" said Wink. His voice was much higher than normal. "They play baseball!" Louder, too. "On real teams! And so could I!" He pounded his fists on his legs. "I could have teammates! I could have friends!"

Hey, you've got a good one standing right here, I thought. But that wasn't what was important right then.

"I'm shorry, shon," said Mr. Wheaton. He crunched the last of the candy in his mouth before continuing. "Things being the way they are . . ." — he tilted an eyebrow in the direction of the corduroy couch and Mrs. Wheaton's housecoat, as if those items were to blame — "it just ain't in the cards."

The wind went right out of Winky's sails, Mrs. Wheaton's housecoat wilted, and even the dancing hula girl drooped.

"Don't they see how you are?" I said loudly to Wink as if his parents weren't even with us in the room, which didn't seem very far from the truth.

Winky didn't speak.

I addressed the slack-jawed members of the couch-committee. "Your son, Elwyn 'Winky' Wheaton, is a miraculous person." They both gave me a look so blank that my brains went boiling mad. I scooped up all the hard candy from the dish in my two hands and threw it at them. They seemed surprised.

"I'm sorry," I said to Winky, and I walked out the door.

Boiled Water Is Not a Good Dinner

I was dragging my feet by the time I walked up the driveway at home. Step-drag, step-drag, scuffing the white rubber fronts of my Keds. I'd won the bet with Mr. Mee on many levels—but still things weren't working out. The sun was lowering, and the way it shone through the leaves and branches of the sugar maple tree behind the garage swept used-car-lot-type spotlights over the fifteen or twenty squirrels leaping around the back steps.

"Get out of here, you stupid squirrels!" I yelled. I picked up a handful of pea gravel and threw it far, and the stupid squirrels went for it as if I'd tossed their beloved peanuts-in-the-shell, a treat that used to be mine! "I hope you choke!" I hollered as I ran up the steps, threw open the door, slammed it shut, and backed against it for good measure.

The kitchen looked exactly like a TV cooking show does not. Pots and pans covered the counter. A row of pasta boxes stood like dominoes on the table. Cans of beans and chopped tomatoes had been opened, their sharp-edged tops sticking up and dripping. Water bubbled in a soup pot on the stove, and from it steam was rising. I put a lid on the pot and turned down the flame under the burner.

"Hi, Grandpa." He was sitting in his recliner in the den, eating dinner off a tray. The TV was on full blast. He hadn't even waited for me to eat his . . . bowl of Oatios with . . . orange juice poured over? As I watched, he picked up a bottle and drizzled some soy sauce into the bowl.

"Grandpa—"

"Shhhhh," he said. He barely glanced at me. "This fellow Brock," he said in a low voice, as if he might disturb other TV viewers, "the one without any shirt, he's threatening to spill the beans about the other one's problem with serial embezzlement, the one in the sarong."

"Brock! Don't speak!" came from the television.

I went to clean up the kitchen. Sometimes when you've had a disappointing day, you're not very hungry, and good thing since all Grandpa had made for dinner was boiled water.

Oh No, Joe

Joe Viola was a terrible disappointment.

The whole town was talking about what happened, and we missed the whole thing because we didn't go to Sunday's game. We had to read all about it in the *Hamburg Catch-up!*

Basically it went like this: Joe Viola was spurned by his girlfriend, a Boston-area nightclub singer whose name turned out to actually be Tina Taylor (no relation to the more famous singer). He'd brought Tina out on the pitcher's mound before Sunday's game (she'd been misled to believe she'd be singing the National Anthem), where he dropped down on one knee and asked her to marry him. The contortions of her face said it all. No, would be her answer. She said she didn't love Joe Viola and she didn't want anything to do with him ever again as long as she lives.

Rejected so publicly, he pitched a stinker and the Hot Dogs lost by nine to the Pennsylvania Dutch. (Their mascot is a grown man in a sailor suit and a yellow wig with blunt-cut bangs. It's more distinguished than Harry the Hot Dog, I guess, but not by much.) Following the game, Joe Viola could be seen cursing at his glove before tearing it apart with his bare hands.

From there the plot twisted like an episode of *The Sands of Time*. Sunday night, according to the fire marshal, Joe Viola entered the sanctuary of the House of Harmony Church by way of the unlocked parish hall door and went in to pray. A deeply religious man, he'd lit a candle. Unfortunately, he was also deeply inebriated. He swept the lit candelabra to the floor and "promptly fell asleep." Evidence shows the fire quickly consumed the velvet drapery sewn by the Ladies' Auxiliary and spread from there. It's a wonder he didn't perish. He thanked the local firefighters profusely, shaking hands all around while at the same time loudly wishing he was dead.

"He had it all," Winky said when I went over to his house Monday afternoon. "He played the great game! Even if it's just for the Hot Dogs." Winky shook his head. "I mean, the guy was born with a *hole* in his heart! He was not a natural-born athlete!" Winky was sitting on the couch beside his father, and had been since I got there.

"Aww, Winky," I said.

"I hate that nickname." He glared at his hands.

"Okay . . ."

"Hate it."

". . . Elwyn."

"Oh, forget it," he spat. Slowly he unwrapped a green sour ball from the candy dish and put it in his mouth.

"He's disillusioned, is what he is," Mr. Wheaton said to me, thumbing in Winky's direction. "That there on that face is dis-il-lusion-ment."

Right then, Winky's face was bunched up into a sad sort of pucker. I thought about how Winky clung to baseball like a lifeline to his true self, the Elwyn-self that maybe he thought was disappearing along with his vision. So there he sat on the corduroy couch. Benched. Awww, Winky.

Winky shifted the candy in his cheek.

"Josie," he said. I thought he might cry.

"Yes, Winky?"

"You should have never. Ever. Touched Joe Viola's glove."

Not a Jinx

I t was all there in the *Catch-up!* Joe Viola had appeared in court on Monday, where the judge set bail at $25,000. The disgraced major league pitcher was taken to the county jail right here in Hamburg, where he awaited trial within sixty days.

I folded the paper and shoved it back in the rack.

"Winky thinks it's my fault! He doesn't want to play ball anymore. And he blames me for Joe Viola's big downfall! He says I jinxed him!"

It was Tuesday, Senior Discount Day at the Pay 'n Takit, and I'd run into Mrs. Blyth-Barrow in the household goods and pet care aisle. We were discussing in general the shocking events of the weekend and in particular the sting of Winky blaming *me* for his idol going to jail.

"He sits on the corduroy couch all day long with his out-of-work dad and sucks on sour balls."

"Josephine, there is no shame in losing one's job," said Mrs. B-B. "I myself have lost more than one." She placed several cans of Frisky Feast in her shopping basket. "Ten percent," she said.

"Ten percent of jobs?" I asked.

"Someone must post ten percent of the bail in order for the prisoner to be released to serve his future appearance. In Mr. Viola's case, that would be $2,500. I studied the law," she explained, "but cooled on the career when my very first case turned sordid—it began as a case of simple embezzlement by a local certified public accountant, and blossomed into murder!" she exclaimed. "It was then that I decided to answer my true calling."

Mrs. B-B smiled. "And I never looked back," she rumbled. (I guess she meant teaching.) "Now then. If Mr. Viola's attorney can reveal exculpatory evidence to demonstrate the fire wasn't set intentionally or with reckless intent, he may plea to a lesser charge or get the case dismissed entirely." She plucked another can of Frisky Feast from the shelf and studied it. "Food for thought," she said.

"Mrs. Blyth-Barrow?" I said. She turned her head and held the can there like she was selling it on TV. "Is there such thing as a jinx?" I wondered if Winky was right. Maybe I'd put the jinx on Mom. I was the reason she and my dad divorced, even! When he knew she was going to have a baby, he took off! And Mom . . . well, she did . . . expire . . . right in front of me.

"Of course there is," said Mrs. Blyth-Barrow.

Oh. I really figured she'd say there wasn't.

"But you are not a jinx."

"No?"

"No. You are not responsible for Joe Viola's problems. It is your responsibility, and everyone's, to be kind; it is your responsibility to work hard and to be curious, but kindness, in the main, is your utmost responsibility. Everything else comes of it. Now, about Elwyn, Elwyn is grievously disappointed, and he's putting his grief onto you—because you, his dear friend, are safe harbor. We often take out our grief on those we are sure will forgive us."

Oh.

"All of this is to say you are not a jinx."

Okay.

"Say it. Josie Bloom is not a jinx."

"Josie Bloom is not a jinx."

"Okay?"

"Okay."

I Visit the County Courthouse

That night I dreamed it was me in jail, with a ball and chain around my ankle. My crime: mail fraud? Check-forging? Nope. Touching a stupid baseball player's stupid glove. The prosecutor wore a "Hello My Name is ELWYN" sticker, and was going for a sentence of thirty-to-life.

I decided to pay a visit to Joe Viola. First thing after breakfast on Wednesday, I walked straight downtown to the county courthouse.

Asa Pike let me go on back to the jail cells—there are two—where my former best friend's former hero sat on a bunk. Talk about a slump.

"Rough night?" I said. He was not looking too sharp in his black-and-white striped inmate uniform. His hair was bushy and dull as rust, and there was plenty of it to be seen, without the baseball cap. Thick stubble covered the lower half of his face, and the upper half drooped with the effects, I figured, of liquor, smoke, and shame.

He eyeballed me blearily. "You again," he said. "This is your fault. You jinxed me. You're bad luck. You put the stink on my glove and my *life*."

Two peas in a pod, this guy and Winky Wheaton.

I thought about what Mrs. B-B had said about me and the jinx. "That's not true," I said. "You were in a slump before you ever set eyes on me, a day I regret for all its dashed hopes and—and *disillusionment*. For making all of my best friend's faith in the game, faith in himself, and friendship with me, go up in smoke."

"I'd like a smoke."

"See, that's what I'm talking about! It's your bad choices that lost you everything. I had nothing to do with it!"

He heaved a sigh. "Whaddaya want, another Sno-Cone?"

"I want you to own up to your responsibility," I said, taking a seat on the folding chair provided by Mr. Pike.

"Responsibility?" He squinted as though he'd never heard of it.

"You're a sports hero to my former best friend. My former best friend is now ruined for baseball. You did that. You put him on that corduroy couch."

"What corduroy couch?"

"The one with his out-of-work father and the sour balls."

"I really want a smoke," he said.

And I really wanted something to say to Winky. Something to restore him to his real self! Something to make him like me again! "Winky Wheaton told me all the wonderful things about you," I said to Joe Viola, ignoring his tone. "The things you've overcome. The hole in your heart!"

"It was a murmur. It went away by itself by the time I was five."

"The selfless things you've done, then. It was like a poem. He told me that you have a heart of gold and the soul of a saint and can throw a changeup like the devil himself. Heck, even my own *mother* kept your baseball card in a heart-shaped frame, right beside the picture of the Pope! You don't live up to any of it!" I declared.

Joe Viola groaned a little and rubbed his chest as if something he ate was beginning to disagree with him. He ran his big hand down over his face. Then he leaned forward on his cot, elbows on his knees, clasped his hands, and hung his head.

"It's true," said Joe Viola to the concrete floor.

I wasn't sure I'd heard right. He might have said, "Itch shoe," which made some sense. He was wearing prison slippers.

He lifted his gaze and stared at me.

"It's true," he said (again, I guess). "What he told you."

"About the hole in your heart? Because you overcoming a disability like that really inspired—"

Joe Viola wheeled his big head to one side and the other like a bear winding up to rip my head off. "No, no, no, no, no, no, no—"

"All *right* already, I *get* it!" I shouted at the exact same time he shouted, "Not *that* part!"

We each took a moment to recover our dignity, me by keeping my eyes and fists squeezed shut. I don't know why, but I started to tear up. Thinking of Winky being mad at me, and blaming me for everything. What did it matter if I wasn't a jinx if Winky believed I *was* one? Winky just wasn't being *Winky* anymore, and it was a little bit too much for me right now, on top of everything else. Just a little bit more than I could hack.

"I meant," Joe said, not yelling (causing me to open my eyes and loosen my death grip), "I did do those things." He pointed deliberately with one finger as if to a clipping in an imaginary newspaper on his lap. "Those things your pal told you I did, all poetic that way."

I sniffed. "You visited the Saint Matilda's Orphanage for Girls?"

He nodded while reaching for a roll of toilet paper.

"You know, I'm an orphan," I told him. "My mother is dead."

"I'm sorry for your loss," he said while he tore off a length of toilet paper.

"You helped out at the Saint Peter's Mission Soup Kitchen?"

He nodded again and leaned to hand me the toilet paper through the bars.

"Soup is good," I said.

"Mm-hmm."

"You were a Big Brother to a boy who lived on the South Side, and that boy always got great seats and free hot dogs and beer nuts at Believers'—"

"Yes, yes, yes, yes, yes!"

Joe Viola really has a problem with repeating himself. I blew my nose.

"Better?" he said.

"A little," I said.

"Listen, Josephine," he said. I looked up. "Right? It's Josephine?" I nodded. "Listen. I wasn't any saint. They made me do all that stuff. For publicity. Management made me up, and your pal fell for the pretty picture in the heart-shaped frame . . ." He flapped one hand weakly and worked his mouth in a way that wrapped hopelessness, disgust, self-loathing, and "go figure" all in one grimace.

His posture crumpled and his hands dropped to the mattress on either side of his lap, lifeless as two fillets of fish. "This is more like it," he said gloomily, indicating with his eyes the cell, his prison get-up, his (possibly itchy) slippers. He did not look that great in stripes.

"I'm sorry about your girlfriend," I said.

He didn't stir.

"That she doesn't love you and that she left you and doesn't want anything to do with you ever again as long as she lives—"

"All right all right all right all right!" he yelled, wicked lively all of a sudden. "All right," he added, collapsing again over his knees. "Thank you."

"Sorry."

I really was sorry for him. Those stripes! They really drove home his situation. Big League star, sent down, disgraced, unloved and—felonious. And in those wide stripes of the prison uniform, he looked like poor old Charlie Brown after Lucy pulls that football out from under him. (Except for needing a shave.) Good grief, Joe Viola.

But still. Winky wasn't wrong. "You did *do* all those things," I said. I thought of Grandpa's plaques. "You Are What You Do," I said, quoting. Winky hadn't any reason to give up on baseball on account of the House of Harmony Church going up in smoke.

But Joe Viola only shook his head. "Number 23 did those things. He was never me. *This* is me."

He heaved a big sigh and leaned back onto his bunk and crossed an arm over his eyes. "Anyway, Tina does love me. She does. She just won't marry me. She found out the hard way I've been married three times. Four if you count that tornado, Mandy."

Mandy! On account of my mom's stories, Mandy is a name that is close to my heart. I paid attention to what happened next.

Joe Viola pushed himself up onto his elbows and laughed the way people do when something's more peculiar than funny. "Three weeks of wedded bliss and then the yelling started." He sat all the way back up and rubbed his face. He shook his head and smiled a little, with one side of his mouth. And then he tenderly spoke that name again. "Mandy."

"Mandy?"

"Mandy," he said, mostly to himself.

There it was again. And my mind went straight

back in time to my mom sitting on the edge of my bed and telling me a story. About a made-up girl who traveled widely and had lots of adventures.

"Mandy Mandolin." I whispered it.

He looked my way then, as if remembering I was there beyond the prison bars. He smiled his little sideways smile. "What a nut she was." He looked at his hands. "Oh, who knows. Maybe we coulda made it."

I became aware of a thrumming sound. Crickets, lots of crickets, or maybe the sound of the blood rushing in my veins and pounding on my eardrums. Woozily, I licked my lips. My mouth had gone dry as Antarctica.

"What was Mandy's last name?" I managed to squawk.

"Why do you wanna know?"

"JUST TELL ME!"

"Okay, okay! McGhee! It was McGhee!"

"McGhee? Are you sure it wasn't *McPheeeee*?" McGhee was darn close to McPhee, Grandma Kaye's clan.

"I'm telling you, the name was McGhee!"

Close enough! "Have you been to Atlantic City?"

"Everybody's been to Atlantic City."

"Wait there!" I said.

"Okay," said Joe Viola. "Since you ask so nicely."

Outside the county courthouse, I started walking slowly. I walked a little faster. Then I started to run.

Believe It or Not

The Sands of Time's got nothing on the Blooms of Hamburg. I ran home practically having a *fit*, and while I ran, I started writing a letter to Ripley's in my head.

Dear *Ripley's Believe It or Not,*

The day she graduated high school, my mother, Cynthia McPhee Bloom, hopped a bus to Atlantic City, where she met one Joe Viola, a famous baseball player, a famous recently *disgraced* baseball player, and they fell instantly in love and got married, but then a month later they split up—over me!—and my mom came back home to Hamburg, Maine, and my dad was *dead* to her—but not actually dead! Then she died for real

and then Grandpa started feeding the squirrels —
so many squirrels! — and the slot machines at the
Chickadee Club, and the water got shut off and I
had to wash my underthings in the girls' *bathroom*,
and then that very baseball player turned up right
in Hamburg and he burned down the House of
Harmony Church and *happened* to mention being
married to a Mandy McGhee, who could only be
one and the same person as —

His Mandy McGhee was my Mandy Mandolin.
And both were *my mom.*

By now I was nearly out of breath. Stop-and-
think. Stop. And. Think. I quit running.

Let's review the facts, I said to myself.

I've got red hair — Joe Viola's got red hair.

My name is Josephine Violet. Joe Viola's name
is — well, it's Joseph Viola.

I can curl my tongue — Joe Viola can curl his
tongue. (That is a *hereditary trait.* I learned it in
science class!)

My mother married some player in Atlantic
City — Joe Viola has been to Atlantic City.

Joe Viola married someone called Mandy
McGhee — my mother told stories about Amanda
"Mandy" Mandolin, and Grandma's family name
was the wicked similar McPhee (so close!).

My mother had Joe Viola's baseball card *still*

sitting on a shelf in a frame—a red plastic *heart-shaped* frame!

Think.

Think.

I doubled over my knees to catch my breath. My heart banged in my chest from the running and the thought of what I knew, I just *knew!*—was true. Charles Dickens himself might have written it! I stood and took a big deep breath.

Oh, Dear Ripley's, I bet anything Joe Viola is my father.

Evidence

Grandpa!"

"Shhhhh." Grandpa was sitting at the picnic table, surrounded by furry friends.

I wanted to sit down—my legs were wobbly and my head felt light. I wanted to ask Grandpa all my questions.

"You ever wonder," he said softly to me, "how they remember where to find all those nuts they hide away in secret?"

I didn't have an answer. But I did have a new appreciation for things hidden away in secret. Or I should say for things hidden in plain sight! I left Grandpa and went inside. I walked straight into the den and to the shelf with the plaques and the pictures. There he was in the red plastic heart-shaped frame, as Brillo–haired like me under that cap as the Pope is Catholic.

I picked up the heart and blew off the dust. I undid the tiny little prongs that held the easel-back in place. I pulled the frame apart and for the first time in my life I saw the back of Number 23's baseball card. In Sharpie was written a romantic message: *You stole my heart XOXO JV*

I knew it, I just *knew* it!

Another Visit to the Bank

According to Mrs. Blyth-Barrow, I needed $2,400. I couldn't let Joe Viola, my own real father, rot in prison. No. I would bail him out, so he could bail *us* out. He *would* help, I just knew it, the way you know the sun will rise and birds will sing. The way squirrels know where they've stored all the nuts. (Though I strongly dislike bringing *them* into my big moment!) The way Winky Wheaton knows his bat will hit the ball. (That's better!) For the sake of those *X*'s and *O*'s on the back of that baseball card, he'd help.

If this wasn't a rainy day, I don't know what is, I figured. I got the Keds box from under my bed and counted the rainy-day money I'd kept. Eighty-four dollars, mostly singles.

I would have talked to Grandpa, I really would have, but he was out, probably sitting on a stool at the Loyal Order of the Chickadee, and I knew better than to turn up there. Leonard probably had the Child Protective Services number taped up by the telephone. So I went straight to the bank to drain the account and bail Joe Viola out of jail.

My mind raced faster than my feet. I tripped on a square of uneven sidewalk and fell down hard, scraping up both knees. I got up and kept on going.

Even though I was hustling down the sidewalk on the outside, inside I felt like I do when *The Happy Painter* comes on TV, wicked calm and peaceful, with an enjoyable tingling on my scalp. It all seemed . . . to fit.

It was not Mrs. Gagne who was pleased to serve me, this time, but Mr. Beebe.

"Certainly not," he said when I asked to make a withdrawal.

"But just the other day, not even two weeks ago, Mrs. Gagne let me make a deposit." The balance in the account at the time had been a whopping $2,614!

"A deposit is one thing," said Mr. Beebe. "A withdrawal is quite another thing." Mr. Beebe stared at me with narrowed eyes, like he thought I was a criminal. Which I was. My stomach urped and my armpits dampened. My eyes raced around honeycomb tile patterns while I tried to think of how I could get at Grandpa's money.

"Besides," said Mr. Beebe, "the account doesn't have sufficient funds to cover such a withdrawal. I shouldn't say it, but your grandfather has only just been here, and he made a withdrawal himself."

I swallowed noisily. "How much?" Was there enough left to *pay* the bail, anyway, even if I *could* get at it?

"Oh, that's private information. I can't say," said Mr. Beebe. "Already I've said too much. I simply cannot say."

It seemed like that was his final word on the subject, so I turned to go.

"Tsk-tsk," said Mr. Beebe, "but he's a regular at the Anchor Bank. The money goes in, and, more often, the money goes out. And on a fixed income too." His puffy cheeks trembled. "The elderly. Such a shame. And yet, I *will* say he always has a respectful salute for the humble bank teller." Mr. Beebe lowered his eyes and put a humble hand to his heart.

Well, this was no good. No good at all. How was my *father* supposed to bail us out if I couldn't bail *him* out? I headed for the county courthouse with all the money I had. It would have to be enough to make something good happen. I just needed to convince Joe Viola of the truth.

Strike Two

I want you to own up to your responsibility," I announced, repeating my line from the first visit I'd paid him earlier in the day.

"Responsibility?" Joe Viola squinted as though he'd never heard of it. Again.

"Fatherhood."

"Fatherhood?" Also apparently unfamiliar.

"Eleven years ago on April twelfth," I explained, "you had a baby girl, me, only you didn't know it."

"Eleven years ago?"

"Yes."

"April twelfth?"

"Yes."

Really, he looked like he wasn't all that swift. He actually scratched his head. "How could that be?" he said.

I took a deep breath and began to explain what I'd learned about reproduction in health class. "When a man and a woman—"

"Never mind!" he said, in a big hurry.

"Look again!" I demanded, pointing. I'd given him the heart-shaped frame first thing, and calmly explained that he was my father, but so far he didn't seem to understand what I'd been telling him. He peered at the picture in the frame.

"No, no, no, no, no," he said. He jabbed the frame with his finger. "That there is a fifteen-cent baseball card available in a million packs of Topps gum. In a cheap frame." He thrust the heart back through the bars and I took it.

"But—"

He held up a stop-sign hand. "You're telling me a couple of *X*'s and *O*'s on a bubble gum card's your proof I'm your father? Kid. I sign a *lot* of cards, every one of 'em suitable for framing. Check the shelves of other ladies in the tri-state area! Come on. That's just—laughable. Haw, haw, haw."

"Well, what about *this*!" I shoved the commemorative keepsake from Maine Medical through the bars. I'd found it in Mom's scrapbook, where she keeps important things like *old Believers programs!*

He glanced at the card. "Yeah, so what? You were born. I agree. Obviously you were born. Nobody's disputing you were born."

I pointed through the bars at the tiny handwriting at the bottom of the card. "What's that say."

He squinted. "Josephine Violet Bloom. So what?" he said again.

"So what? So what?" I grabbed a bar in each hand and spoke slowly and clearly. "Your name is *Joseph Viola.*" I thumped my chest. "*My* name is *Josephine Violet.*"

Joe Viola went very quiet. He went a little pale. Then, he opened his mouth, and he said, "That is thin. That is wafer-thin."

"Mandy McGhee was my mother!" I said, making two fists and stamping my feet.

"Says right here your mother was Cynthia Bloom."

"But she used to tell me bedtime stories about a girl called Mandy!"

"So what? My momma told me stories too, doesn't mean my pop's Rip Van Winkle!"

I grabbed two fistfuls of my own hair and yanked. I breathed deeply. "Listen to me, you—you felon!"

He shrugged. "I'm kind of a captive audience, here."

I breathed deeply again. "My mother ran away to find herself when she was eighteen years old. She was away for eight weeks, and then she came home and then nine months later I was born."

He picked at his thumbnail.

"And she used to tell me bedtime stories about a girl called Amanda Mandolin, who traveled to exotic places and had lots of adventures that always ended happily."

"Happy endings," Joe said, "well, there's the proof there's no connection to me."

"You were married to my mother, Cynthia—" I stood.

"Kid—"

"And she had a baby but didn't tell you."

"Kid—"

"She must have wanted to be someone else, to be Mandy—"

"Kid—"

"Because she told me Amanda Mandolin was a real *character*, a girl who traveled widely and had lots of adven—"

"Kid! Stop! Stop it stop stop stop!"

I stopped, not because he told me to but because I was out of breath.

He was shaking his head slowly, as if it was very heavy and full of something that went side to side, such as sand, or oil, or a Magic 8 Ball. "Believe me," he said, "I was never married to any Cynthia woman."

"But—"

"I never had any kid."

"But—" I ran out of things to say. The face of Joe Viola was so blank, so confuzzled, as Grandpa would say. Was he a drinker? I'd heard of people having blackouts, where they lose entire blocks of time. . . .

"Look at me," he said. "Do I look like anybody's father?"

"Plenty of fathers are incarcerated," I said, "don't be snobbish. Plenty of fathers burn things down and pay the price for their—their passion!"

Joe Viola sighed like a soap opera star and dropped down onto his bunk.

I held up the red plastic heart-shaped frame, with his younger self wearing Number 23. "I don't know what you think the game of baseball is all about," I said to him through, yes, a blur of tears, "but Winky Wheaton says it's about connecting. The eye and the ball and the bat and the heart." I banged fist to chest two beats, right where it hurt. "That's right, Joe Viola, you arsonist," I said, "the *heart*."

"Oh, I know all about the heart," said Joe Viola. He sprang up from his bed and strode to the bars and gripped them in knuckled fists. "I loved her with all my heart," he said, a moan really, while looking me straight in the eye. Oh! Here it was at last! The truth! "I *loved* her!"

"My—my mother?" I blubbed.

Joe's face went all twisty with sorrow. "No, not your *mother*," he said. (Okay, not sorrow, then.) "For the last time, kid, I never heard of any Cynthia Bloom, let alone in any scenario with me wearing a monkey suit and going on a honeymoon in Vegas!"

"*Atlantic City!*"

"No!"

"Liar!"

"Whatever!" He thrust a hand through the bars and Mr. Pike half rose from his orange plastic chair down the hall, but sat again when Joe Viola withdrew his hand. But there was his face up against the bars, looking every bit the mug shot.

I would have asked my mother why she ever married such a liar and all-around insensitive person as Joe Viola in the first place, but, of course, I couldn't. I reached into my sweatshirt pocket.

"Well, I guess you won't be needing *this* from your *daughter*," I declared, and flapped a stack of Grandpa's money under his nose. It wasn't anywhere

near the full $2,400 bail, but he sure got the idea.
He brightened right up. A look of love came over
his face, but I knew it was only for the money.

"Forget it!" I said, flapping the bills again
before stuffing them back in my pocket.

"Kid!" he called after me, but I was already
gone.

"I'm not your kid, according to *you*!" I hollered
over my shoulder.

Winky Does Not Believe It

I called Winky. So what if he was mad at me and thought I'd put the stink on his sports hero and ruined them both for baseball. I needed my friend.

I explained everything. Winky didn't say anything, but I felt his friendship and understanding very strongly through the phone line.

"So I think he may be in shock," I told him. "Heck! He didn't know!" I said. "It's perfectly understandable he finds it hard to accept that he's a dad, *my* dad, and with his own recent and very public heartbreak, plus his near-death experience at the House of Harmony Church . . ."

I reached into my pocket and wrapped my

hand around the bail money. "It makes a lot of sense that he doesn't understand what I'm telling him. And we don't look all *that* much alike, really, other than the hair and the freckles. Do you think? I think it's mostly in the eyes." I stopped talking and the line was quiet.

Winky finally spoke. I wished he hadn't. "Josie," he said, "it's a stretch."

I hung up on Winky Wheaton. Then I banged the phone a couple more times for good measure. Then I kicked the phone table and hurt my foot.

I hobbled up to my room. I flopped on my bed and buried my face in the pillow and imagined being dead till I had to lift my head and take a gasping breath. I sat up and looked at the little red plastic heart-shaped frame on my bedside table. There was my father's—my *father's*—*XOXO*, framed there in that heart, the way they say in love songs on the radio it was written on my mother's heart, on *my* heart. Maybe the reason I felt so bad was more than needing help. Maybe it was more than needing money.

And Winky Wheaton! How could he not believe me? How could he do that to me? Winky, of all people, my best friend. I flopped on my tummy again and buried my face in the pillow again and imagined being dead again. Then I fell asleep.

Some time later, I woke with a start. Grandpa was home—I could tell from the lively game show noises clanging and ringing from the TV downstairs. I sat up. I had to try again. Just like Mrs. Blyth-Barrow had told me to. (She was talking about my poor grades and absence of homework and my *ennui*, whatever that is, but still.)

I *would* try again. I would make Joe Viola believe me. I would march right back there with my good-faith money and make him believe the truth. Because once he believed me that he was my father, then all my problems—Grandpa, the money, the old folks' home, the orphanage—all my worries, well they'd go right up in smoke, the magic kind, not the cigarette or arson kind. Poof!

Three Strikes

I bounded down the stairs to tell Grandpa the big, big news. I hoped it wouldn't give him a heart attack.

"I have something to tell you," I said to Grandpa. Luckily, he was already sitting down. Not luckily, it was his reclining chair, and he was wicked involved in a TV game show.

"Shhhh," he said, without even looking at me. "If this gal answers correctly, the money is hers!"

Well, I didn't have time to wait around.

I said goodbye over the clangs and gongs of *The Money Is Mine!* Then for the third time that day, I went to the county courthouse.

By now it was near four o'clock, and the sky

was heavy with summer heat. Clouds were as big and messy and billowy as my hair.

I marched straight to the courthouse door and gave it a good push. Nothing happened. Then I remembered to *pull*. I marched down the hall, since Officer Pike was not at his station. As I neared the corner where I'd turn to go down the hall to the jail cells, I heard voices (*mumble-mumble four-seamed fastball!*) and then laughter (*haw-haw-haw!*).

I rounded the corner and saw Winky Wheaton sitting on the edge of his seat (*my* folding chair!) outside Joe Viola's cell. Asa Pike was leaning against the wall, his arms crossed over his chest and looking like he'd just chuckled. All three of them stopped and stared at me.

"What are *you* doing here?" I said to Winky.

"Well, you went to see him, and I got to thinking I owed it to myself to ask him what I wanted to know. I asked him what went wrong, how could he throw it all away, the great game? And he said he'd made bad choices." Here Winky turned to Joe Viola, who lowered his head and lifted his hand like he was the Pope. It was an obnoxious display of pure fakery. Bad choices? *I* told *him* that. "He's humble," Winky said. "I gotta respect that."

I rolled my eyes. Then I got back on track with the line I'd planned on opening with, before I got thrown off by Winky being there. "Well, *I* am here to visit my *father*!"

Asa Pike chuckled, Joe Viola groaned, and Winky Wheaton turned bright red, as well he should have.

Viola said, "For the last time, kid, I'm not who you want me to be! I'm sorry—"

"You sure *are* sorry!" I said at the top of my lungs—

Joe Viola shrugged. Then he yawned.

"Oh, you're bored?" I said.

"Yeah! This is unbelievably boring!"

"No, *you're* boring! You just mope around in here feeling sorry for yourself!"

Asa Pike cleared his throat.

"It doesn't make any sense!" Joe Viola said.

"It makes perfect sense!" I said.

Winky touched my arm and said, "Josie."

"Don't you touch my arm, Winky Wheaton," I said. I turned on him. "You're stupid!" How could he sit there and touch my arm and leave me hanging out to dry like that! I thought my head would explode like that lizard I read about in *Ripley's Believe It or Not! Reptiles Edition*. (It grew back!) "Nothing could be stupider than a blind kid being in love with a game he can't even see! What a waste!"

I reached into my backpack, pulled out all the

good faith bail money, and threw the wad in Winky's lap. "Here!" I said. "Waste it on the stupid playoffs!"

Winky studied the stack of cash, turning it over in his hands and holding it close to his face to get a good look. "But you just said nothing could be stupider than a blind kid being in love with base-ball. You just said, big waste of money."

"I can think of a bigger one," I said, glaring at Joe Viola.

Already I was regretting my show of defiance and generosity. (The two are not natural partners.) The truth is, I didn't really want to give Wink the money. I needed it. I needed to bail out Joe Viola so he could, as my real father, keep me out of the orphanage and take care of everything. I couldn't do it. I needed things I didn't even know I needed. Would the bank take our house? Mr. Beebe had all but told me Grandpa's broke!

"This money smells bad," Winky said. He sniffed. "Fishy." He held the money out to me. "Smell it."

I saw my chance and took it. "You don't want my stinking money? Fine!" And I yanked it right out of his hands. "I think I've made my point!" I hadn't made any point, but at least I'd got back the money. "Goodbye!" I said bravely.

"I'll walk you out, Josie," said Asa Pike.

"No, thank you," I said. As soon as I rounded the corner in the hall, I slumped. The money, and Amanda Mandolin, my mom kissing me goodnight, the smell of her Wella Balsam shampoo . . . I heard Asa Pike's footfalls coming down the hall. *Openopenopenopen!* I whispered to the door as I tugged. Then I remembered to *push*, and out I went.

A Sign at the Cemetery

I ended up in the cemetery.

Cynthia McPhee Bloom. I ran my fingers over the letters. The carving still felt new and deep.

"I'm right about Joe Viola," I said to Mom's gravestone. "Aren't I?"

Aren't I?

I sat right down on the grass. A raindrop hit my arm. Then a few more drops pattered around me on the ground. Maybe Winky was right, I thought. Maybe I'm bad luck. A jinx. Or maybe I need money so wicked bad that my words and deeds can't be trusted. You Are What You Do, it said on Grandpa's plaque. I'm a check-forger who hangs around in shady clubs and prisons.

Maybe I'm making Joe Viola into my father, I thought. Making him up just like he says Management made up Number 23. Maybe, I thought, I want a dad just the way Winky wants a hero, and we both think Joe Viola's him, but he isn't.

But—isn't he? I was so sure, and then I wasn't.

I was feeling sorry for myself, just like how I'd accused Joe Viola.

I'd misremembered my *tarte tatin* memory. Did I misremember the daffodil memory too? Was I *not* someone who could take care of things? Was Mom wrong to think I was better than I can ever be? If Grandpa goes (goes to the Home, goes squirrel-crazy, goes to jail for illegal gambling!), then I don't have anybody, is what I was thinking.

Then I heard, "Josie!"

It was Winky. He was holding a bunch of flowers, plastic ones. I watched Winky come across the cemetery. I thought about him and his ever-present baseball glove when he was little, and what he'd lost and what I'd lost, and how we were lucky to be friends. We *are* lucky. He'd said so. And he was right. That much I did know.

He handed over the flowers and we stood there like stones, if stones could have hearts and those hearts could ache.

Winky cleared his throat. He pointed at the

flowers. "I brought those 'cuz I'm sorry," he said at the same time I said, "I'm sorry I said you're stupid."

We both went quiet again, but now it wasn't so achy.

Flash! Heat lightning.

I counted, slow. One, two, three, four, five—

Rrrrrummmmmmble . . .

The sound of thunder. The storm was five miles away.

"I thought I was low when Grandpa didn't pay the oil bill," I said to Winky. "I thought I was low when I found that first big mortgage statement. I was *wicked* low when Becky caught me doing laundry in the girls' bathroom."

Winky just nodded. There wasn't really anything to say. Mom's gravestone sure wasn't helping.

I dropped down and flattened myself full-length on Mom's grave, I don't know why. At that moment I was in every way as low as I could go. I need a sign, I thought, any sign. Please, somebody send me a sign!

Just then, an eerie wail deafened my ear, a warm wind blew oily fumes to my nose, and the earth rumbled beneath my entire body. I pushed myself up on my knees like a person about to pray or throw up.

Then I saw the Peter Pan bus grumbling toward us along Pine Street, destination BOSTON, and plastered big as life on the side of the bus as it passed was Peter Pan himself, pointing the way.

And then it started pouring warm, soft rain.

The BBL

It was a sign," I said to Winky. We were sitting side by side on the Peter Pan bus, heading south on I-95. That's right, we were Boston-bound. "Maybe from my mother."

Winky pulled on his chin. "Mrs. Blyth-Barrow says the dead are with us. She has a lot of knowledge about world religion and the occult."

"Did she used to have a minister-job?" I wondered.

"Maybe," Winky said. "She's had a lot of jobs. Maybe sorcerer."

Here's what happened: I still had the eighty-four dollars in my pocket. Joe Viola had refused to believe the truth. Winky had come and stood by me when I was wicked low, which is what he really always did. I thought of what Mandy Mandolin would do, and I did it.

"Your sports hero's in a slump—that's right," I said, hopping up from Mom's grave. "The slump of all slumps! He's in jail, for Pete's sake!" I smacked Winky in the arm, with the plastic flowers. "The Believers aren't going to the playoffs. Forget about the playoffs. Us two, the two of us, we are going to take this money, and we are going to Boston this very Saturday on the Peter Pan bus, and we are going to the Boston Beep Baseball Bash," I announced.

We went straight from the cemetery to Winky's house. Mr. Wheaton was the first to speak from the couch. "How're you gonna pay Peter Pan? You can't have a penny from Brenda's Book Cozies. We require every last cozy penny for ourselves!"

"Right you are, Bob," said Mrs. Wheaton.

Mr. Wheaton clasped his hands behind his head, thereby thrusting forward the design of his sweater, a machine-knit summer-weight number featuring an owl in flight across the great golden moon that was his belly.

"Never you mind," I said, lofty like a lady on *The Sands of Time*. "I've got the money." I whipped out the good-faith bail money and smacked my palm with it.

Winky gasped. "But what about Joe Viola?"

"That bum?" said Mr. Wheaton, bringing his arms down and ruffling the owl's feathers.

"That bum can rot in prison for all eternity! I couldn't possibly care any less than I do!" I said. I was doing very well with the dramatic delivery, I thought. I tossed my head like a horse for good measure. Mr. Wheaton seemed impressed. His mouth dropped open. Then, noticing the opportunity, he put a sour ball in it.

The Wheatons agreed to let Winky go to Boston on the bus and go to the Beep Ball Bash as long as it was "scot-free" and as long as we were accompanied by an adult who was "not us." Grandpa, too, agreed to the trip, but wasn't up to going. No problem. We told the Wheatons that Grandpa was going with us, and we told Grandpa that the Wheatons were going with us. So here we were, just me and Winky, alone and on our way to Boston. Sure, it was sneaky. Yes, we lied. But it was barely a blip on the lie-o-meter. We had it all planned out so nothing could go wrong.

The first thing to go wrong was we got lost right outside the bus station. Hamburg has Maine Street,

and the other streets go off of that one in a likely sort
of pattern. Boston hasn't got a Maine Street or even
a main street. It has lots and lots and lots of streets.
It hasn't got any kind of pattern we could figure.
Cars were honking and drivers were hollering out
their windows at each other. A grubby-looking old
man was just sitting on a stoop. He smiled at us, but
he didn't have any teeth. He asked us for money.
When I got close to give him a quarter, I noticed
he smelled like he took even less baths than I did.
There were lots of people walking and hurrying.

Luckily, we got so lost we went in a circle and
ended up at the bus station again. I went in and
got a little map from the guy at the ticket counter.
For free! And it turns out we were even closer to
Fenway High School than I'd thought. Wicked!

The next thing to go wrong was when a policeman stopped us.

"Where are your parents?" he said.

I kind of stammered, but Winky thought fast.
"They're parking the car. We're all going to Fenway
High School because of the Beep Baseball tourna-
ment going on there. Because I'm blind."

The policeman brightened right up. I have
noticed that sometimes people go out of their way
to be nice and helpful to Winky once they notice
he's blind. And when this happens, and people are

wicked friendly and want to lend a hand, Winky isn't all that thankful. He doesn't even always act polite!

"Well, what you wanna do, is, you go straight down the end of the block, here, right on Elm, left on Wickham . . ." The policeman didn't talk in slow motion, like some people do, like Joe Viola's girl-friend did, that time, when they realize Winky can't see. "Well, see here," said the policeman, "I'll just walk you there myself, no trouble at all."

That would sure be trouble for us, though.

Just then I saw a man and a woman getting out of a car up ahead. "There they are!" I said, and I waved. After a little hesitation, the lady waved back. "See?" I said to the policeman. "We'd better catch up to Mommy!"

I grabbed Winky's hand and started running. "Bye now!"

Sure enough, we found our way to Fenway High School. Once at the field, we sat on the sidelines with what seemed like friends and families of the players. We'd missed the first game of the day, but another game was in full swing.

We sat down where there was some space on the grass, beside a lady in an orange T-shirt who was the kind of person who likes to talk a lot. We introduced ourselves, and she told us she was married to the right fielder. She pointed to a chubby guy wearing a black blindfold that looked like one of those little Halloween eye-masks, with the itchy elastic that goes around your head, only without any holes to see out of. He had on a baseball hat, and sweatpants, and a team jersey that said Boston Bats.

There were six fielders, all wearing blindfolds, and two guys out on the field who weren't wearing blindfolds. I explained all this to Winky, and then I asked the orange lady, "How come they're wearing blindfolds, if they're blind?"

"Well, it's so everybody's got the same level of vision. My husband is completely blind, can't see at all, but other players have some sight, like you, Elwyn," she said, and patted his hand, "so the blindfolds make everybody's vision the same: zero.

"Now, there are those two players on the field that don't wear blindfolds, and those are the spotters, and they're sighted. They'll call out where the ball's headed, once it's hit. 'Course, the pitcher and the catcher are sighted folks too."

A player from the other team, the Holyoke Hawks, got up to bat. He was kicking his cleats in the dirt and fussing with his hat, and everybody went quiet as Sunday service.

She whispered in my ear. "We have to simmer

down so the batter can hear the ball," she said.

The pitcher being a sighted person made sense. The pitcher being on the same team as the batter made less sense, till I saw how it works.

"Ready!" the pitcher yelled. Then he threw the ball. We could hear the ball beeping on its way to the batter.

"Swing and a miss," I whispered to Winky after the first pitch. The catcher tossed the ball back to the pitcher.

The next ball was a hit. A spotter yelled out "Two!" and orange lady's chubby husband stuck his glove out, but missed. "Typical," his wife said. There was a lot of yelling and then another fielder got the ball.

While the fielders were trying to get the ball, the batter was running pell-mell straight for the base. The base was this foam-encased upright thing about as tall as me, and it buzzed the whole time the runner was running toward it.

The fielders got the ball before the runner got to the base, so he was out. And that was the end of the inning. During the changeover, the lady explained how it works.

The game is played with six fielders and one or two "spotters" from one team, and the pitcher, catcher, and batter from the other team. The ball is a modified softball that beeps. Batters time their swings—and players field the ball—by listening for the beep. When the ball is hit, the batter runs to one of two bases located at about the positions of first and third base in regular baseball. The base buzzes when a base-operator turns on either one of them and it keeps on buzzing while the batter runs for it. Meanwhile, a sighted "spotter" yells out the number that indicates the part of the field the ball is headed for. If the batter touches the base before the ball is fielded, it's a run. If not, it's an out.

The way she rattled off the rules, you'd have thought she wrote them herself. "You sure know a lot about it," I said.

"Well, you go to every game, like I do, you pick it up pretty quick. Naturally, there are nuances," orange lady said.

"Naturally," Winky said.

I always thought regular baseball was boring. This was different. This was wicked exciting. Maybe because we were right on the sidelines, and maybe because the orange lady was so friendly. But probably mostly on account of my idea and my wish that Winky might actually be able to play baseball again.

There was another game after that one, and after *that* game was all done, orange lady said, "Come on and meet Coach Bart."

Winky was going all nervy again, like he did when he met stupid Joe Viola, a person I did not want to think about. I wasn't about to let this go. We'd come all this way and we weren't leaving without Winky getting what he came for. Or getting what I wanted Winky to have come for.

Coach Bart was a bowling-pin-shaped man, wearing a stretchy, zip-neck shirt with wide black-and-white stripes. His shorts were black, and also stretchy. Good thing, because he did a lot of bending of knees while he talked, and he even hopped up and down a couple times.

Coach Bart took out a handkerchief and patted his sweating, red face. "Join us!" he said to Winky. "We take all comers," he said, "providing you're to some degree blind."

"Stargardt disease," said Winky. "But even *I* can tell there are stripes on your shirt."

"That's why I wear it," said Coach Bart. "To aid and assist my players, off the field. 'Course, during play, they're all blindfolded."

We all mumbled a little, how people do when they don't know each other very well.

Winky said, "Our teacher once coached a winning slo-pitch softball team to a pennant in Punxsutawney."

Coach Bart hopped. "She interested in a job?" he said.

"Well, she's already got a job," Winky said.

"But maybe we could talk her out of it!" I said. I was already thinking how great it would be to have a teacher who didn't threaten to take steps.

"Whattaya say we give it a go!" Coach Bart said to Winky. And this was the very best part of the day. Winky went up to the plate and put on a blindfold. He dug his toe into the dirt. He brought the bat up high.

"Ready!" called Coach Bart.

Winky hit that beep ball, first try. Orange lady threw the switch to make a base buzz, and then— okay, *this* part was the best—Winky ran!

The crowd went wild! Sure, I was the only person left in the crowd, but I yelled my head off. "Go, Winky! Yayyyy!"

It was a good day. A great day. I glanced at Winky in the window seat of the Peter Pan bus, heading home. He still had a big smile on his face. The Beep Baseball League had put it there. But I'd helped.

All Is Lost

The sun had gone down and the sky was deep dark blue when the bus rolled into Hamburg. We said our goodbyes at the station, feeling like more than just one day had happened. I didn't even flinch when Winky gave me a big hug. I knew it was coming because he had already thanked me fifty times for sneaking him to Boston. And the whole entire adventure had gone off without a hitch. It couldn't have gone any better if Amanda Mandolin had planned it herself!

They say everything looks different after a day of success. I don't know if anybody really says that, but that's what I was thinking. It felt good that I helped Winky get back, in a certain way, something he'd lost. Wicked good. I'd barely thought about Joe Viola all day! I strolled past the school, happy as a clam. The recess field was full of pretty dandelions. Dandelions everywhere! Yellow ones, and also ones all gone to puff and ready for wishing on.

Those bills for the mortgage and things aren't so much, really, I was thinking. Grandpa gets checks that go *into* his bank account, sometimes—it isn't all money going *out*.

Walking by the Pay 'n Takit, I waved to Mr. Miller. He waved back and I saw his mouth go, "Hi, Josie!"

Leonard from the Chickadee Club wasn't going to call Child Protective Services. No way! If he was, he'd have done it by now!

I glanced over at Books 'n Things, and saw myself in the window, wearing my new baseball hat. I'd splurged on one for me and one for Wink. I straightened the bill, and gave myself a thumbs-up. Lookin' good!

Grandpa's fine! He's dandy! Slot machines aren't so horrible. Lots of people gamble. It's entertaining! And the blurting? Blurting is normal! There's nothing wrong with a blurt every now and then. Lots of times, the words even make sense, sort of!

I came to the corner of Portland and Maine,

and the air smelled smoky, like a BBQ on the Fourth of July, right when you squirt the lighter fluid onto the charcoal briquettes. A patriotic song came to mind, and I hummed a little of it. Humm—hum-mmhmm—humm-de-dummm . . .

I crossed Maine and cut through the parking lot of what had been the House of Harmony Church, and that's when I heard the siren.

I ran after the fire truck, top speed, because that's what you do with a fire truck. You run and see what's the emergency!

I chased that wailing fire truck all the way up my own street and my own block and—

Oh no—

my own driveway, and—

I could barely see the house—

billowing smoke. No!

Orange flames. Crackling hissing roaring.

Thumping—my chest.

Pounding—my ears. No!

"Grandpa!" Gasping. "Grandpa, Grandpa, Grandpa!" Coughing.

A huge, faceless thing loomed up and blocked my way and shovels came down on my shoulders. I screamed. The thing lifted a shovel to its not-a-face and pulled off—a mask. It was a person, a firefighter, and he steadied me with a heavy gloved hand on my shoulder. "Stay back!"

He moved aside and then another firefighter stepped through the smoke-and-flames—something big and lumpy heaped over his shoulder.

"GRANDPA!"

Beanbag Hands

Maybe if I'd stopped to make a wish on one of those dandelions at the school, this wouldn't have happened. Maybe this, maybe that. My mind spun crazily, sickeningly.

I pulled my new baseball cap practically down over my face and squeezed my eyes shut tight. I had snuck away to Boston, and Grandpa could have *died*! Chief Costello was patting my head, and it was making me cringe.

"It's only a house," Chief Costello said. "Only walls and a roof. Your grandpa's okay. Everyone is safe. No firefighters were hurt. Maybe the house can be restored. My wife's sister runs the show over there at Disaster Blasters. You'll see. Good as new."

Just then, the roof caved in.

"Nonsense, Chief Costello," said Mrs. Blyth-Barrow. "That house is a goner." She put a hand on my shoulder. It felt gentle and firm at the same time, like a beanbag. I felt my hunched-up shoulders release a little. My forehead, and my jaw. I breathed in, I breathed out. Nice, comforting beanbag. I closed my eyes and shut out everything going on around me: the dying fire, gray smoke lit by all the headlights, the shift and boom of the ruins, the ambulance, the noise of the firefighters and EMTs, the sound of Grandpa coughing, someone saying, "There you go, Martin, that's good, you're all right now, you're gonna be all right," and underneath it all, a low, soft, three-tone humming. Hm-mm-mmm. Hm-mm-mmm.

But then a stab of pure mean shot through me and my eyes snapped open—from smoke, from tears, they *stung*: All I did was go to Boston to do something good and nice for my friend, and Grandpa up and—Grandpa—and *this* happens!

I looked at Grandpa, where he sat in the back of the ambulance, breathing into an oxygen mask. Oh, Grandpa! Chief Costello said Grandpa was okay, but was he? Was he really?

The humming went away. Mrs. Blyth-Barrow lifted her beanbag hand from my shoulder, and before I knew what I was doing, I reached up and grabbed it. I needed that steady, gentle weight on my shoulder. I needed it, or else I might tip over and fall right down. I turned into her, and she put her arms around me. That three-note humming started again; it was Mrs. B-B humming to me, like someone would hum to a baby in the night.

Standing there with Mrs. B-B's arms around me tight, rocking back, forth, my cheek against her soft sweater, I felt a lot of things — guilty, and angry, and sorry and scared . . . Everything rolled through me and over me sort of like when you know you're going to throw up, and then you do throw up, and then you feel weak, but better. Like that. Then I felt calm. Even peaceful.

There's nothing I can do, is what I was thinking. The cat is out of the bag. It's all gone up in smoke. I can't take care of it. It isn't possible to take care of it. Someone is going to have to take over now. I didn't know what to think about that, except that it was true.

And Mrs. B-B just kept on holding me, and holding me, and she didn't say one word, not one, about me getting gunk on her special sweater.

Mrs. B-B Takes Us In

Here's what happened. With me off in Boston, Grandpa had tried out a new recipe for dinner:

Step 1. Put water in pot on stove.

Step 2. Forget it till firefighters appear.

Mrs. Blyth-Barrow took us in.

It was late—close to midnight—when we climbed the stairs to Mrs. Blyth-Barrow's apartment over Kenerson's that night. The first thing I noticed was a large statue of an angel in her living room. It was about three feet tall, with the wings, and her arms reached in front of her like someone had stolen a bouquet she'd been holding. I was as tired as I've ever been in my life. I rubbed my eyes and looked at that angel again in case I was seeing things.

"Lovely, isn't she?" said Mrs. B-B. "She will eventually go on my grave. Death is part of life. It's another change. A big one, I grant you."

The biggest.

"I operated a bed-and-breakfast for three glorious years in Glastonbury," Mrs. B-B said, moving on, "and I still maintain a tidy guest room, though it be humble." She dipped her chin, very humble. Then she threw open the door on a room blooming with chintz and ruffles and needlepointed pillows. On the coffee table sat a vase of fresh flowers on a doily and a floral-printed hardcover boxed set titled *Jane Austen: The Complete Works* (also on a doily). She swept her hand toward twin beds with matching bedspreads.

"Popcorn!" said Grandpa.

"Yes, that's right," said Mrs. B-B. She patted one of the bedspreads. "Popcorn-chenille. Such a discerning eye," she said. "Sleep, now, and try not to dream. They're sure to be nightmares."

It smelled just like a bakery when we woke up the next morning. And when Grandpa and I came out of the guest room, there was Mrs. B-B in the kitchenette, wearing a ruffly apron and pulling a sheet of scones from the oven. "The secret is a bit of orange zest," she said to Grandpa. He held his chin and hmm-ed like it was an interesting tip that he would definitely try out as soon as possible.

After breakfast, Grandpa sat down in the overstuffed chair by the living room window, and spent some time admiring the upholstery, an explosive pink print featuring what Mrs. B-B said were cabbage roses. He plucked at the protective cloth on the rolled arms.

"Antimacassar!" he blurted. Several of Mrs. B-B's cats padded over and surrounded Grandpa, where he sat looking not quite like himself in the chair that wasn't his recliner. He scratched one cat behind the ear while another cat took up a spot at his shoulder, on top of the chair. Loud purring came from all around. I don't like to see so many cats in one place, but it was a step up from squirrels.

I curled up on the chair's matching loveseat and spent a long time staring at the first page of the first volume of the Jane Austen boxed set. At one point in the afternoon the doorbell rang, and when I went downstairs to answer the door, Becky Schenck handed over a paper bag full of clothes.

I was surprised. "That was really nice of you," I said. I didn't want to wear her castoff clothes.

Still, it was a surprise to see Becky here at the door being friendly. For the first time ever, I smiled at Becky Schenck. "Thanks, Becky. This really means—"

"It wasn't my idea," said Becky. "My grandmother died around Christmas and we still have all her crap. The granny-panties *are* actually my grandmother's underwear. And the blue smock will look good with your frizzy hair and blotchy complexion. Because it's ugly."

There's the Becky Schenck I know! I smiled again, or I should say I stretched my lips to show my teeth. "Thank you so very much, Becky!" I said, and closed the door right in her face. It felt really good. If only I hadn't needed the clothes, I would have shoved her granny's panties in the dumpster out back.

The doorbell rang again, and this time it was Bubba Davis at the door.

"Did anybody die in the fire?" he wanted to know. He had a bag of Lay's potato chips and he was eating from it and staring at me with big eyes like he was at the movies and I was on the screen.

"No," I said.

"Anybody end up in the burn ward?"

"No."

"Anybody faint?"

"No."

"Hospital?"

"No."

He reached into the bag of Lay's and ate a handful of chips.

"Disappointing," he said.

"'Bye, Bubba," I said.

Winky came over to keep me company awhile, but said he didn't want to come into our teacher's apartment. "I really don't. That would just be wrong," he said. "I might see things I could never unsee, and I'm blind."

The day passed in slow motion. "The day after excitement or tragedy often does," said Mrs. B-B. What questions I thought of to ask, I didn't know if I wanted the answers to. What I wanted to tell Grandpa—about me and Joe Viola and Mom and Mandy Mandolin—I couldn't, because I was afraid of how he'd take it, being so worn-out from being rescued from a burning building, and all. So I poked around the bookshelves and listened to Grandpa talk to the cats (I finally got an accurate count—eight—and filed the number away to report to Winky), and the three of us played a board game called Aggravation that really lives up to its name. At four thirty I set the little dinette table for dinner (old people like to eat early), and we had just sat down to find out what cottage pie and wedge salad are, when the doorbell rang again.

Prize Winnings Are Determined

Mr. Mee looked different outside the school library. He looked like a Sears mannequin in his off-duty clothes: tan Bermuda shorts, navy-blue Keds, and a yellow polo shirt.

"You don't look so persnickety in that outfit," I said when I answered the door. "Respectfully."

"I am precisely as persnickety as ever," he said. "I went by your house."

Rainbows, butterflies, soup. Every time I thought of the house—the flames, the smoke, and Grandpa on the firefighter's shoulder—I tried to think of something else.

Mr. Mee was staring at me over his glasses.

"Sometimes," he said, "I like to look at a thing and ask the Universe: Why?"

For such a tiny word, "why" is a big, huge question. It should be spelled with about twenty *y*'s on the end. Whyyyyyyyyyyy. My knees suddenly felt rubbery, maybe because I'd been going up and down the stairs so many times. I kind of collapsed on the stoop, and Mr. Mee sat beside me. He set down by his feet a paper bag from the Pay 'n Takit.

"Did you get any answer?" I asked him. "When you asked the Universe?"

"No. I never do. But sometimes it's enough to ask. It's a way of paying my respects to Chance, who cares nothing for winning and yet is always the victor. I accept that."

I thought about what he'd said for maybe a full minute. "Is that sort of another way of saying nothing really matters because everything goes up in smoke in the end?"

"More or less," said Mr. Mee. "But you make it sound so pessimistic. It's *realistic*."

"Right." I saw the flames again in my head.

"But then, there's this." He reached into the paper bag and pulled out a ruler-length of charred wood. It was one of Grandpa's plaques. Plenty of extra wood-burning on it now, I thought. "Maybe this explains why we can face uncaring Chance, again and again, with a brave face," said Mr. Mee.

I took the plaque from him and read it. "'Hope Is the Thing with Feathers.' I never really got this one."

Mr. Mee nodded. "It's the first line of a poem by Emily Dickinson." He took a breath.

"You're going to recite it, aren't you," I said.

He laughed. "You know me well," he said, and adjusted his glasses. "Hope is the thing with feathers—that perches in the soul—and sings the tune without the words—and never stops—at all."

"That's nice," I said.

"And sweetest—in the gale—is heard—and sore must be the storm—that could abash the little bird that kept so many warm."

"Okey dokey—"

"I've heard it in the chillest land—and on the strangest sea—yet—never—in extremity, it asked a crumb—of me."

Mr. Mee stopped talking. From somewhere near came the call of an actual thing with feathers, which was kind of wicked, considering.

"Is that the end?"

"Yes, that's the end," said Mr. Mee. "I thought you might like to have it," he said, and pointed at the plaque.

"What I'd really like to have are those prize winnings we never determined, for finding a fact you didn't already know." Not that it really mattered anymore. "About the Beep Baseball." He didn't say anything.

"Don't tell me this plaque is my prize," I said.

I waited.

"Do not tell me that," I said.

"Okay, I won't tell you."

I sat there on the stoop of the Five and Ten after Mr. Mee left, with the plaque in my hands. The plaque smelled of smoke and ashes. I know I should have been full of hope and everything. But I wasn't. And then that bird called again, and it was loud and sharp and not a bit sweet, a blue jay probably, the bully of the backyard bird set. It sounded just like Becky Schenck.

I Make Like Amanda Mandolin

When I got back upstairs, Mrs. Blyth-Barrow was just hanging up the phone. The cord was long enough that she could walk all over the apartment while talking on the horn, and she had wound the whole length of it around her wrist. It took about a minute for her to free herself.

"That was a Mr. Lincoln of Child Protective Services," she said. "He would like to set up an appointment to talk to you both—to all of us, in fact—as soon as possible." She looked at me in a stern way. "To help, Josephine. He wants to help."

Yeah, right. Foster care? The System? I didn't want to live with strangers. What if they made me move away from Hamburg? Ooh, that Leonard, I thought. I could wring his neck, if I could reach my hands around it.

If that phone call wasn't enough, right after that I spotted a pamphlet on the telephone table. It was just like the one I found that time in Grandpa's secretary, the one with the pictures of the old people clinking their wineglasses, the vegetables and so forth. I guessed Grandpa and Mrs. B-B had been talking about the Home. I guessed she was taking steps.

"What do you have there, Jo-Jo?" Grandpa said. He was looking at the plaque with the burn marks.

"Nothing," I said.

I went into my flowery room and plopped down on the popcorn-chenille. From there I chucked that plaque across the room in the neighborhood of the little yellow trash can. It missed, and made a racket.

"What's going on in there?" said Mrs. B-B.

"Nothing!" I hollered. *Leave me alone!* is what I *wanted* to holler.

That plaque might as well have burned up in the fire, for all I believed it. There was nothing hopeful here. Grandpa was going to the

Downeast Best Rest, and I was going into Child Protective Services.

I stared at the ceiling. What would Amanda Mandolin do? Mandy Mandolin was brave and adventurous. She sure as heck wouldn't sit around in Becky's granny's underwear, waiting to be hauled off to live with strangers.

I sat up. I knew exactly what Mandy Mandolin would do. She had done it before.

The ticket agent at the bus station had no problem taking my money. Grandpa's money, I mean.

I'd written out a check and forged Grandpa's signature like old times, only I made the check out to me. I'd seen Mr. Miller cash a check for Grandpa before at the Pay 'n Takit, so I figured it could be done. Sure enough, a man with a toothpick in his teeth and a plastic nametag on his chest cashed the check at the Plaid Pantry.

"Thank you, Billy Bob," I said, wicked polite. I tried not to sound like I was getting away with something.

"Aw, that ain't my real name," Billy Bob said, tapping the nametag. He switched the toothpick to the other corner of his mouth. "I just made it up."

If that wasn't a sign, I don't know what is.

"Interesting," I said. I left that store with a spring in my step. If I had a nametag on, it would say: AMANDA.

I went straight to the bus station. I knew the drill by now, after buying tickets to Boston—was it just yesterday? The day before that? The station agent took one look at me and said, "Boston?"

I shook my head and looked up at the board with all the destinations on it. Boston, Wabash, Nashua, New York. If Joe Viola refused to believe he was my father, then fine. I would go and look for more evidence to prove it. A marriage license, a kind stranger who might have been the witness to the wedding . . . something.

Grandpa was going to the Home, and it was just like Winky had asked me that night we found Grandpa at the Chickadee Club. If Grandpa went to the Home, then what would happen to me? I didn't want to have to go and live with a bunch of strangers. I wanted a family. *My* family.

"Atlantic City, please," I said, and handed over the money.

"Doesn't head that way till tomorrow, sweetie," said the lady.

"Oh." I looked again at the board. Nashua, New Hampshire, was the next bus departing Hamburg.

Nashua, New Hampshire, was not the destination I had in mind. Nashua, New Hampshire, was not helpful.

What-to-do where-to-go how-to-prove-it. Questions chased each other around-around-around like a cop-car light in my head—and then, for the second time in a week, I heard the siren.

I Go to the Pokey

The next thing I knew, I was sitting in the back of Asa Pike's police cruiser. There was a barrier between the front seat and the back seat, made of wire mesh. I felt like I was already in prison.

When I'd heard the siren blare, I'd turned quick and there was Officer Pike in his police car. He did a "cheers" with his Dippin' Donuts cup, but it wasn't a friendly one, I could tell. His eyes were narrowed. Sure it was a sunny morning and he might have been squinting. But the squint, and the way he smiled at me—too wide to be really friendly—and how he sort of *pointed* at me with his coffee cup . . . obviously he was suspicious. I could only hope he'd drive on by.

He rolled down the window. "You going some-where?"

Had Mrs. Blyth-Barrow called in a miss-per? Had the police put out an APB? These are terms I knew from TV and never thought would apply to any situation *I* was in. It was the end of the line already. I had watched enough police shows to know.

"I'll go quietly," I said to Officer Pike. "There is no need for force."

"Good to know," Officer Pike said. He didn't get out of the car, but I knew what to do. I opened the back door and climbed in.

"Okay, then," said Officer Pike.

I shut the door. The vehicle started moving. We rode a block in silence. We stopped for a pedestrian at the corner. Officer Pike waved the pedestrian across. Then who should walk by on the sidewalk right alongside us but Winky Wheaton. Officer Pike waved to Winky. Winky waved back.

"Goodbye," I whispered to Winky. I put my hand up to the glass, which was around two inches thick. Apparently, Winky couldn't bear to put his hand up to mine. He couldn't even look at me, poor guy. I looked out the back window as the cruiser pulled away, but the seat was kind of high and I was too short to see much. Winky was probably standing there sadly, watching me roll away.

Officer Pike was chewing a donut that magically appeared. I could see him in the rearview mirror. He was silent as the grave. I would know.

I couldn't take it. I cracked.

"Then you know about the gambling?" I said. My throat closed up, and there was a pressure in my chest, just like that time a butterscotch candy went down the wrong pipe. I don't even like butterscotch. "You know about the money? The checks? The trespassing? The grave robbing?" My voice was strangely loud and clear and ongoing. "The bank? The forgery? The bar? The lies?"

Officer Pike seemed to be having a lot of trouble swallowing the donut. Then he reached up and moved the mirror a little, and after that I couldn't see him anymore. I stared out the window at the town, my town, going by. Beautiful Hamburg. Beautiful, beautiful Hamburg. Would I ever get to walk freely to the Pay 'n Takit again? Officer Pike was taking the scenic route, driving up and down every block. Looking for troubled kids, I guessed.

We drove past Winky's house. The TV was on in the living room. Then on to Unexpected House. Hey! There was a big pickup truck parked in the driveway, and the front door was wide open! For the first time ever! The cruiser rolled on by before

I could see who was inside. I sat back in the seat
again. My eyes teared up, they truly did. Now I'd
probably *never* know what was happening on
Desirable Street.

What about school in the fall? Was there a TV
at the courthouse? I hadn't noticed when I had visited Joe Viola those times. I wasn't thinking about
TV back then. Now I thought I would miss it quite
a lot.

The drive to the courthouse was probably the
longest four minutes of my life. When we got there,
I was cold, but sweating, and that hard lump of
butterscotch in my chest hadn't melted at all.

I peered out the window of the cruiser. I'd
always thought the courthouse looked like a castle,
what with its three stories of sparkly granite, and
those columns and the big windows. Now the building's true, grim nature showed itself to me. It was a
prison. For breakers of the law, like me.

Suddenly my view was blocked by a dark
blue shirtfront with a badge on the chest. The door
opened. "You comin'?"

Asa Pike led me into the building and down
the hall to the cells. He nodded to Joe Viola, in the
first cell. Joe raised a hand weakly. I guess that's
what happens, here, I thought. You weaken.

Any reminders of better times were gone. There

was no aroma of Asa Pike's lunch coming from the kitchenette. The vending machine was nearly empty. Gone was my folding chair outside Joe Viola's cell. Gone, gone, gone. Officer Pike opened the door of the second cell. "You can have a seat in here, Josie," he said.

I nodded.

I went in. The door swung shut behind me.

"I'll be back," he said.

I sat down on the bunk. I figured I'd better save my strength.

A couple long minutes went by.

Want to know how time passes in jail?

Wicked slow.

Joe Viola got up from his bunk. He stepped to the wall of bars that separated the cells. Our eyes met, and what passed between us was the kind of understanding that only two prison-mates share.

Then Joe Viola burped. "Urp. Sorry. Salisbury steak." He thumped his chest.

And I started crying my head off.

Turns Out I Am Not Actually Arrested

I know you don't believe me," I blubbed. I dragged my sleeve under my runny, snotty nose. "But I am *positive* you are my real father, and I need my father, so if you could just"—*hic!* Great, now I had the hiccups!—"just believe me. I need you."

Joe sighed. "I won't say 'and I need a smoke,' because I can tell you're pretty emotional."

Blub-blub-blub!

"Hey, now," he said, "it's going to be all right, you'll see."

"How do—*blub*—*hic*—you know?" *Blub-blub-blub!*

I was about ready to sock him in the nose,

but one look at his face and I didn't want to anymore. He was looking sadly at me. Like I was a little puppy he thought was helpless and didn't know any better than to pee on the carpet.

"I'm not a—*hic*—puppy!"

"'Course not," Joe said. Not mean. Okay.

I blew my nose and *hicced* a few more *hics*.

"Hey," Joe said, "you know it's not necessarily so great having a full set of parents. It depends."

I honked my nose again.

"My parents split up when I was about your age. What are you, eighteen, nineteen?"

I sat up a little straighter. "Eleven."

He nodded. "Ah, right, eleven. My ma used to buy me all kinds of stuff she couldn't afford. I was the first kid in the neighborhood to get a whole little suitcase set of Matchbox cars!"

"That sounds nice," I said.

He frowned. "Yeah. And then *he'd* buy me *more* stuff. First kid in the neighborhood to sport a three-piece *suit*!" He snorted and shook his head. "Stuff was just to get back at each other, and cover up they didn't want to have a thing to do with me. Our house was a battleground, I'm telling you."

"That sounds crummy," I said. No kid wants to wear a three-piece suit, for example.

"But I always had this thing inside me, this

important thing," Joe went on. "I always had base-ball, and the game, the players, the coaches—those people were more like family. And that place became my home. Know what I mean?"

He made a sort of *pffff* sound, like a balloon emptying that last little sad bit of air, and he lowered himself onto his bunk bed like a tired old man.

"I guess I got a new home now," he said. "Got all I need, right here handy."

I stared through the bars at him. I needed my mom. I needed my house not to have burned to the ground. I needed Grandpa to quit feeding all those squirrels and slot machines. I needed money and time and a plan and Winky Wheaton's faith. All I had was Emily Dickinson's hope, and that was just a little fluffy bit of stupid . . . poetic . . . fluttery . . .

"Quit feeling sorry for yourself!" I said, all of a sudden. I jumped up. "I need Number 23!" I said. I actually stomped my foot. "I need—" I covered my mouth because I thought I might cry again, and I spoke through my fingers. "I need help. I thought you would help."

Joe Viola didn't even straighten up one inch.

"Kid," he said to his striped kneecaps, "I guess you're outta luck."

I sat back down on my bunk, and the two of

us were quiet for a minute, just breathing and sitting there. We sat there a couple more minutes. He had no place to go, of course, and I didn't either.

Then Asa Pike came waddling down the hall wearing the Harry the Hot Dog costume and a fanny pack. "I'm doing double duty today at the game," he said. "Mascot and Security." He zipped the fanny pack, patted it, and swiveled it around the back of the buns. "To hold the cuffs," he said. "You'll be okay?"

He pulled up the puffy foam hot dog hood and cinched it under his chin.

"Will I be *okay*?" I said. "Isn't there some paperwork you have to file?"

"Paperwork?"

"For my arrest?"

He looked very seriously at me, and pressed his lips together, hard. Then he said, "Why, you're not arrested, Josie."

"I'm not?"

"You're free to go."

"I am?"

"Ayup. So long as your grandfather doesn't want to press charges, that is."

Asa Pike made a big show of pulling open the unlocked cell door using only his pinky. "I was driving around on my coffee break and saw you someplace you might not oughta be, and picked you up and"—he shrugged—"you did the rest."

Joe Viola didn't laugh, I'll give him that.

Then Asa Pike noticed something down the hall beyond the cells. "*There* you are, you ole thing," he said, and he went and grabbed the folding chair and came back and unfolded it for me. "Have a seat. Your grandpa is on his way."

I sat.

"You'll be okay?" Asa Pike/Harry the Hot Dog asked again.

"Yes." How embarrassing. "Fine."

Asa Pike/Harry the Hot Dog waddled away.

Inside his cell, Joe slumped over and rubbed the back of his head with both hands, kind of moaning, and mumbling to himself things like, *I'm all washed up. She isn't coming back. I'm outta the league. I'm done. I'm cooked.*

I knew how he felt. I didn't have a mom. Joe didn't think he was my dad, or else he didn't want to be my dad—either way meant I was an orphan. An orphan! And Grandpa was not ever going back to the way he was before the blurting and the saluting and all that started. The house was history. It had been a long day already. And it had been what they call *humbling*, being released from jail by Harry the Hot Dog. Humbling, and—silly. I started to laugh.

Joe Viola straightened up and looked at me like I was nuts. Then I cried *again*. I cried really hard, for a really long time. Joe kept stretching his hand through the bars and trying to reach me and saying "Hey, now," and "There, there," and then I inched closer and he was patting my shoulder and my head, sometimes missing when I tipped one way or the other from the force of my tears.

After a while I started to feel like I might be cried out, and then I really was cried out. I was feeling a little better, and it looked like Joe Viola was feeling worse, kind of moaning again, and sighing like a steam iron.

That's maybe why I remembered a story I read about in *Ripley's Believe It or Not! Crimes and Misdemeanors Edition*, long before I took up visiting people in jail. It was about an inmate in an Oklahoma prison. He married twelve different lady-visitors, one after another, while serving out a sentence of thirty-to-life.

I was thinking about that Oklahoma inmate being so lonesome he married twelve ladies, and how Joe Viola would probably do just about anything for a chance to get his girlfriend back, when Grandpa and Mrs. Blyth-Barrow came charging down the hall.

I stood up. "You want to press charges?" I said

to Grandpa, knowing by now it was a joke.

"I certainly do!" he said.

"No, you don't," said Mrs. B-B.

"Certainly not," Grandpa said.

"Come along, Josephine," Mrs. B-B said. "We have lots to discuss, and you must be hungry. We saved you some breakfast."

"Crumpet!" said Grandpa.

"I'll be right out," I said.

Grandpa and Mrs. B-B headed back the way they came. I waited till they disappeared around the corner. Then I stepped right close to Joe Viola's cell, and gripped the bars, and looked straight into his red-rimmed eyes.

"What'll you give me if I can get your girl-friend to come and talk to you?" I said.

"No way, no how," he said. "Uh-uh, nope, not gonna do it."

"You big baby," I said. "A big tough baseball player like you ought to be able to do it with your eyes closed and your hands tied behind your back!"

"Oh, my eyes will definitely be closed," he said, "and they'll *have* to tie my hands behind my back!"

"So you'll do it?"

"No!"

"If it isn't true," I said, ignoring him, "if the

blood test shows you're not my real father, then I'll go away and no harm done and sorry I touched your glove that time, and it was nice knowing you."

We'd learned all about this DNA testing thing in health class, and I knew it was *possible* to get that test done . . . maybe not likely . . . but maybe . . .

He looked at the ceiling of his cell and then he smiled a little. "It *has* been nice knowing you, sorta," he said to me.

"Thank you."

"I mean you're not that bad."

"Okay."

"For a kid."

"Joe," I said, serious as a heart attack. "If it *is* true, if you are my real father . . . well . . . wouldn't you want to know?"

He looked at me a long time. He ran a big hand over his face and then he nodded. "Yeah. I guess I would. But I'm not. And even if I am, Josie, there's nothing I can do for you. I'm broke, I'm no good to anybody, I'm all washed up."

He flopped down on his bunk and crooked an arm over his eyes. "Be careful what you wish for."

Pajamas!

I wish . . . oh, everything's changing," I said.

We were back at Mrs. B-B's apartment, and she'd brought out some lemonade.

"Naturally. Everything changes," Mrs. B-B said. "Change is life's only constant. Look at my hair! Do you think I was born with this color?" She folded her hands in her lap. "I miss my husband," she said. "Howard was a kind and gentle man who up and followed me hither and yon wherever my jobs and enthusiasms took us. Howard had a hungry mind and a pleasant disposition. Yes. I miss him every day."

It's strange when you learn something private and personal about your teacher. I didn't know what to say about Howard, so I said, "Your hair is really nice."

"Thank you."

"It's very . . . bright."

"Miss Clairol number seventy-one, and Aqua Net Atomic Hold. Change is good! You lose things — jobs, husbands. Houses. But if I were a betting person" — she shot a look at Grandpa — "I'd bet you gain much more than you lose."

I thought about Mom. I thought about Winky and his eyesight and Beep Baseball. I thought about Joe Viola. Then I sat down on the flowery loveseat and I told Grandpa and Mrs. B-B everything, the whole story. I didn't have anything to show, I didn't have any proof. What little I'd had — the baseball card in a red plastic heart-shaped frame and signed with X's and O's — burned up in the fire.

They listened. The cats purred. Want to know what eight cats purring sounds like? Wicked sympathetic.

When I finished talking, I glanced at Mrs. Blyth-Barrow. She hadn't moved an inch. I knew she'd once been an artist's model, and that she could sit perfectly still for thirty minutes at a time.

"Do you . . . believe me?" I asked.

Grandpa stood up. "Coincidence Is Fate's Favorite Tool," he said.

"Who said that?" I had never seen that saying on any plaque, but I thought it deserved one.

"I did," Grandpa said. "Didn't you recognize my voice? Pajamas!" he added.

"Of course we believe you believe it," said Mrs. B-B. "But we don't have to theorize. Perhaps you don't know that I once was employed at a medical laboratory in Portland, and through connections I maintain in the field, I understand the new method to test paternity is based on the analysis of human leukocyte antigens . . . quite accurate, affordable, and quick."

"I thought of that!" I said.

"Of course you did, Josephine. You're no dummy." Mrs. Blyth-Barrow scooted away a large marmalade tabby from under the end table. "Shoo, Pajamas," she said.

Whole Lotta Love

Joe gave me Tina Taylor's number, and I called her on the phone. I told her I was the kid she met on the field, the one who touched Joe Viola's glove ("You!" she gasped), and that I had something wicked important to talk to her about.

"It's Joey, isn't it," she said.

"Yes," I said.

"Is he sick? Is he dyin'?"

"No, no, nothing like that."

"Too bad," she said.

Not that I asked, but she told me Joe was a three-time loser in the marriage department—

"Four-time," I said, but she kept talking right over me—

And how he didn't trouble himself to *share* that information, and how he was a gall-dang liar and sure there were good times, *puh-lenty* of *good times* (her voice turned all low and drippy, euw) but if you can't trust a man to inform his potential *wife* that *that* role has been previously filled *three* times—

"Four"—

"Well, then you can't trust him as far as you can throw him, am I right?"—

"Well—"

"You know it, child, and speaking of children, for all I know, he's got a *pack* of kids"—

"Just the one"—

"And can I tell you somethin'?"—

"Uhh"—

"I *want* a pack of kids! And Joe says he doesn't want *any*! Says his childhood was a horror show, what with the hole in his heart"—

"Murmur, went away by itself"—

"And his folks not being exactly top-notch and him leaving home when he was just a little squirt, but you wanna know somethin' else?"—

"Uh-huh"—

There was a pause.

"I can't help it," Tina said. "I love the big jerk, just how he is."

I didn't want to ruin the love-spell, so I didn't say a word.

"And I think I can change him," Tina added, wicked heartfelt.

You'd have thought she was all talked out, but she agreed to come and talk to me in person at noon on Thursday.

Tina pulled up in front of Moody's Diner in a rusted yellow Mustang with the top down and the music blaring. The music quit but the car seemed to want to hang on, chugging and shuddering and ticking while she fussed with her hair and made it the big perfect cloud it was the last time I saw her, at Hot Dogs Field. Then she unfolded herself from the driver's seat and slammed the door with a hip-check.

"Here I am!" she sang, tugging down her little skirt. "And there *you* are. Don't touch my stuff," she said with a straight face.

We went inside and took the booth on the end, and if anybody thought it was odd to see me splitting a big slice of coconut layer cake and a hot dog with a glamorous stranger who some say looks like famous singer Tina Taylor (and who *is* Tina Taylor, no relation), they didn't say so.

Well, I did get Tina to visit Joe Viola in jail.

How? By telling the truth. But telling it *slant*, following advice I took from another one of Emily Dickinson's poems, which I read some of, out of Mrs. Blyth-Barrow's bookcase. Mrs. B-B and Mr. Mee have similar taste in poetry. (Ha! A poem, right there.) I'm not sure about the romance novels.

The slanted part was that after I explained to Tina how I was Joe's daughter—

"Little jinx like you?"—

I swore that he loved me with the part of his heart that wasn't already devoted to *her*—

"Sweet Jesus!"—

And that he eagerly accepted his responsibility—

"Sing it!"—and wanted to change—

"And I'm just the one to change him!"

I told the truth so slant it was falling over, but I think I made Emily Dickinson proud.

My story seemed to make Tina very happy. She cried noisily, putting her hands over her face for privacy, and I took the opportunity to finish the coconut cake. It was delicious. Then Tina stopped crying, finally, and took her hands from her face. "Is my mascara okay?" she said.

Wow.

"Probably could use a touch-up," I said.

Tina Taylor's yellow Mustang was still chugging and ticking and taking up two spaces in the parking area of the county courthouse when she strode right by Asa Pike and straight to Joe Viola's jail cell as if she had a homing device. Two minutes later—two minutes of nonstop talking by Tina, and Joe Viola saying things like "Yes, I do" and "Whatever you say" and "Well, we'll see" and "A pack of 'em?"—they were hugging and kissing through the bars, euw.

Tina waved me over to join their hug-fest, but Joe and I both said things like "No" and "Errrrr" and "Let's wait for those test results."

Ye Olde Scientist

Seventeen Days Later,
Not That Anybody Was Counting

By then Joe Viola had been in the county jail for twenty-eight days. Tina had been staying at the Motel 7 out on Route 4, and she kept taking me for slices of cake and hot dogs at Moody's Diner, and sometimes Grandpa and Mrs. Blyth-Barrow would come with us. Tina got to having dinner with us at Mrs. Blyth-Barrow's apartment—"Four thirty p.m.? That's not dinnertime, that's cocktail time!"—and teaching me songs in the car. I agreed to let her do my hair—"I'm dying to!" she said. She said if we cut it and "went at it with the hot rollers," it would "get up in a ball" like hers instead of looking like "saggy bell bottoms."

And I had gone to visit Joe every single day, whether he liked it or not.

"Oh, he likes it all right," said Tina.

I'd told Joe Viola all about me—about Mom, and Winky, and Grandma Kaye, and Grandpa, and Becky Schenck, and all the summers and all the school years—everything he'd missed because he didn't know he had a daughter right here in Hamburg, Maine.

So there we were, Tina and Joe and Winky and Asa Pike and me, all crammed in cozy in Joe Viola's cell at the county courthouse, eating fried chicken from Moody's—"Prison's no picnic, but we can have a prison picnic," Tina figured—when Rex Grigg, the postman, delivered the mail.

Mr. Grigg walked right on in—Asa Pike didn't even lock the jail cell door anymore—and he was waving an important-looking envelope over his head. He was wearing the postal-service-issue pith helmet. (Say *that* five times, fast!)

"I believe you've been awaiting this missive?" said Mr. Grigg.

My heart started banging in my chest. I couldn't believe it was finally, really happening. We were about to find out. I was frozen to the spot.

"Paternity test results?" Mr. Grigg said.

That unfroze me. "Hey!" I said. "What do you know about it, I thought the US mail was supposed to be private!" I said. *People in Glass Houses Shouldn't Throw Stones* came to mind, although that wasn't one of Grandpa's wood-burned mottoes.

"Well, it *is* private, sworn duty, neither rain nor snow and all that. But you see, Vera Bean told me, and Ben Miller at the Pay 'n Takit told her, and Sandy at the Dippin' Donuts told him, and let's see, I guess it was Debbie over to Moody's told her, and Leonard at the Chickadee, he knew, and said something to Chief Costello, and—" Mr. Grigg took his pith helmet off and wiped his forehead with his wrist. "There you have it. Arrest me."

He held out the envelope. I took it. My hands shook.

Then Mr. Grigg did something surprising. He squeezed his eyes shut and bowed his head and crossed all his fingers on both hands and put them over his ears like he couldn't stand to hear but also wanted to very much.

Tina grabbed both of Joe's hands with both of hers. Asa Pike dropped his chicken drumstick in the bucket and pressed his hands together like he was praying.

I looked at Joe Viola. He looked . . . scared?

Hopeful? I couldn't tell! I kind of lifted my eye-
brows at him. *Ready?* He squeezed Tina's hands.
Then he nodded. And he smiled. *Ready.*

I stood there looking at him. I wanted to tell
him how I hoped he really was my dad. I wanted
Tina to know I liked her, too. But it was even more
than that. I loved them already. I did. I already loved
them! I—I—I swallowed a big lump in my throat. "I
just want to say—"

"Open it!" everybody said at the same time.

So I did. I opened the envelope and took out
the paper inside.

But I couldn't unfold the letter. I didn't dare!
What if I'd been wrong all along and Joe wasn't my
real father? What then? What would happen to me?
Where would I go, where would my home be? My
knees went all rubbery, and I sat down on my folding chair.

I held out the paper to Joe. He shook his head.
Tina? She shook her head too. Then Winky put out
his hand. "I'll do it," he said.

Winky held up his magnifier and looked the
whole thing over, and I swear nobody took a breath
for about three and a half minutes. It's a wonder we
didn't all pass out on the floor. Finally, Winky let
the magnifier drop. He folded the paper.

"He's not your father, Josie."

Earth never was a piece of the sun. Wasn't that what Mr. Mee had read out of that *Book of Knowledge*? I had a pretty good idea of how ye olde scientist felt the day he learned that what he'd believed—what he'd really, really believed, with all his heart— wasn't true.

9-1-1

Mr. Grigg left on his rounds. "I suppose other citizens will want their mail delivered today."

Officer Pike went to the little courthouse kitchenette to do the dishes; we could hear some sad little clinky sounds, and the water running; running, yes, *like tears*!

Tina took off to Moody's to order an entire coconut layer cake; "It'll cheer us up," she said. And then it was just me and Joe Viola.

It was real quiet.

How could I have been so sure, and so wrong?

Joe said, "Well, I told you, didn't I."

I nodded, although I didn't want to.

"What a relief!" he said.

"Thanks a lot," I said.

"I'm not a person who'd be a good dad, Josie. But thanks for thinking I would be. I could never take care of a kid. You're better at taking care of things than I am," he said.

"You don't know what you're talking about," I said.

"Well, I'm in here, and you're out there, for one thing."

He was so wrong. He didn't know how wrong he was.

"What, you don't buy it? You don't think you're good at taking care of things?"

"There are things you don't know," I said.

"I know you helped your buddy get his game back."

"It's not like I invented the BBL."

"You managed to pay your grandfather's bills."

"Not very well!"

"You took care of your grandfather when he couldn't take care of you!"

"No, I—I left town and the house burned down! He might have died!"

"Listen, I'd be *proud*, I'd be *very* proud. I mean if I *was* your father, Josie, I'd be—"

"I didn't call immediately!"

"What?"

"Mom! My *mom!* I just stood there and stared at her, and all the time she was—her heart was giving out. It was giving out right in front of me! I just stood there! I didn't move or say what you're supposed to say, which is 'I love you,' or even breathe! I—"

"Josie—"

"I didn't even know what was happening!"

"That's right, Josie. You didn't know."

"But—"

"You were nine years old, just a little kid. How were you supposed to know? Hey, nobody knew your mom had a heart condition."

"I didn't take care of her," I said, "and that was my only job."

"It wasn't your job. That job is not—it's not age-appropriate. Your job was to be a kid. Go to school, do your chores, eat your peas and carrots." I didn't say anything. "Look, I'm not exactly father-material, as we both know, but I'm pretty sure I'm right about this one."

I thought about that.

I thought about that a little more.

"You wanna hear a story?" said Joe.

"Yeah," I said. "Okay."

Joe Viola leaned forward. "It was June the seventh, 1971. Believers at Flyers Stadium in

Weehawken. I'm pitching a no-hitter, Believers up by four runs. I get the first two batters with weak ground balls. Then I strike out the third batter, but the ball squirts away from the catcher, and now there's a man on base. The next batter leans into the pitch and it's a reach with a hit-by-pitch. A walk to the next batter loads the bases. Things are going south on a greased pole."

Joe leaned back and drew a hand over his face like he was mopping off fresh sweat. "Then I go and give up the grand slam with two outs in the bottom of the ninth to tie the game. The manager takes me out at that point and sends in a relief pitcher to get the final out of the inning, and that sends it into extra innings."

Listen, I was pretty tired. I yawned.

"The *point* is, Josie," said Joe, "the game wasn't over yet. It wasn't anywhere near over! There were extra innings." He put a lot of emphasis on *extra* and *innings* and looked at me, hard.

"What does that mean?" I hoped it didn't mean that this story, which was wicked boring, was going to go on much longer.

Joe spoke very slowly. "It means, sometimes the game has to go into extra innings, before it's done."

I thought about that. I might not read much besides *Ripley's*, but I know a *metaphor* when one hits me over the head with a baseball bat. He meant I needed to hang in there. He meant I needed to be patient and see things through. "Did you win that game?" I said.

Joe Viola crossed his arms over his striped front. "Well, I'm just not going to tell you, am I, because you were so bored by my story."

"Oh *come on!*" I said. "Tell me if you won!"

Joe didn't answer me, but he looked pretty smug, so I'm pretty sure the answer was yes.

Extra Innings

"E xactly as you predicted," I said to Mrs. Blyth-Barrow.

We were at the diner, Mrs. B-B, Grandpa, Tina, and me, finishing up breakfast. Mrs. B-B was reading aloud from the *Hamburg Catch-up!* The paper reported how Joe Viola's attorney eventually revealed exculpatory evidence to demonstrate the fire at the House of Harmony Church wasn't set intentionally or with reckless intent. The judge dismissed the case entirely in exchange for Joe Viola agreeing to community service. Sentence reduced to time served. He got out that very day.

Before Joe was let out, I went to see him one last time. The courthouse jail had been like home for the both of us, and neither of us had another home to go to from there.

"What's going to happen to you?" I asked him.

Joe rubbed his face. His red hair stuck up. "I don't know. I need to *think*. You *know* I'm no Number 23 anymore, not that I ever really was." He scratched his chin. "But what would Number 23 do?"

It was then that I had a wicked good idea. I stood up so fast the folding chair collapsed, as if it knew its services would no longer be required.

"I will settle for Number 5," I said.

"Huh?"

"Number 5 will be good enough for my purposes."

Joe smiled a little. "Your purposes? What're you gonna do, harvest my organs? You need a kidney?"

"I need somebody who looks good in stripes."

"Stripes? What do stripes have to do with anything?"

"Patience is a virtue," I told him. Now, *there's* a motto to make a person suffer.

"So I've heard," said Joe Viola.

I had some work to do before I could share my idea. It might not work. But it might.

The Home

"Home is where you hang your hat," Grandpa said.

The day I'd feared and dreaded for most of sixth grade had finally come. Insurance had paid off the house. There was no more mortgage to keep track of or pay. I was staying with Mrs. B-B because, well, I didn't have any place to go. And Grandpa was moving into the Home.

Grandpa hooked his blaze-orange hunting cap on the back of the door to Room 7 at the Downeast Best Rest. It was a two-room suite, not too bad. Someone would clean it, and someone else would make his meals. Those people would not be me. I felt a little happy about this, and also sad. It had been just Grandpa and me for long enough that I didn't know how else to be.

At first I blamed Mrs. B-B for moving Grandpa into the Home. I was mad. But I remembered what she had said when Winky blamed me for Joe Viola's downfall, how Winky did that because he was grieving and I was what she called safe harbor; he knew I would forgive him. It was the same with Grandpa moving. I was really sad and scared to see Grandpa move into the Home. I couldn't be mad at *him*, but I could be mad at Mrs. B-B. I was a real jerk.

"I'm sorry," I told her.

"Have a cookie," she replied.

"Hobnobs!" said Grandpa. He seemed happy enough.

Then he headed off to the activities area, probably to the wood-burning station to make himself a new plaque.

Mrs. Blyth-Barrow and I went to the cafeteria and we each got a pudding. She got the banana pudding and I got the tapioca pudding. From our table in the dining room, I could see Grandpa in the activities area.

"This is a good place," Mrs. B-B said to me. "And I'll be right here, most days," she said.

I looked at her. BALITHIA BLYTH-BARROW. She had on a nametag. So did I. Everybody at

Downeast Best Rest wears a nametag, right out in the open. It's nice. It's like the opposite of a Brenda's Book Cozy.

"I've quit teaching," I thought I heard Mrs. B-B say. That couldn't be right.

"What did you say?" I said.

"I've taken a part-time job here at Downeast Best Rest. Activities director." She held up a hand as if to stop me. "No, no, I don't need a fat salary," she said, not that anybody asked. "You'd be surprised how much money I've socked away," she told me, "gained largely during my brief but almost criminally profitable stint as a stockbroker." She took a big bite of banana pudding.

I had complained about my teacher all year long, but now I felt a lonely hole somewhere around my stomach. This was maybe one thing too many. I started to tear up. Again! "Is Mr. Mee still librarian?" I managed to ask her.

"Yes, of course," she said. "I'm done teaching, but I'm still here, Josie." She tugged a tissue from inside her shirt cuff and handed it across the table to me. "I'm not going anywhere."

Mrs. B-B put down her spoon and patted her tummy. Then she pushed her dish of banana pudding across the table. "I'm too full to finish," she said.

And so I ate the very last bite, and it was delicious.

Later, I went and sat beside Grandpa in the activities area. He was, in fact, using a pointy tool to burn words onto a piece of wood. The smell of the wood burning was kind of comforting and nice. Like a crackling fire in a fireplace. It smelled like a holiday.

"Want to make one?" Grandpa asked. He elbowed me a little in the ribs. "You can never have too many motto plaques."

I did not agree with that. Still, I poked through the basket of suggested sayings.

Home Is Where My Cat Is

Time Spent with a Cat Is Never Wasted

A Cat a Day Keeps the Doctor Away

"There sure are a lot of cat mottoes," I said. That last one didn't even make any sense.

Grandpa pointed at a lady helping over at the scrapbooking table. She was wearing a smock made out of fabric with cats printed all over it.

"That explains a lot," I said to Grandpa. I pulled another slip of paper from the basket.

Love Is Spoken Here. Meow! Ick.

Home Is Where the Heart Is. I kept that one out. If that's true, I thought, then I would have to live at the Downeast Best Rest too, and it is really no place for children, much as I enjoy pudding of all kinds. I pressed the motto on the table and smoothed out the creases. I kept smoothing it and smoothing it and smoothing it. I stopped when Grandpa put his hand over mine. His hand was freckled and dry and warm.

"Grandpa? I love you," I said. I don't know why it was so hard to say, but it was. I said it pretty fast.

Grandpa sat up ramrod straight and gave a snappy salute. Then he took both of my hands in both of his. "Ditto," he said. His mouth worked around a little. "What I mean to say, is, Josie, is . . . love is . . . my heart is . . ." Still holding both my hands, he leaned and kissed my head. "I mean I love you too."

Unexpected House on Desirable Street

The rest of summer passed the way it always had—twenty-four hours in every day, seven days in each week, the hours and the days and the weeks dragging and also, somehow, zipping by.

We had a pretty good routine, me and Mrs. Blyth-Barrow, while I waited for what would happen to me next. Child Protective Services allowed me to stay put "in the interim." Saturdays we'd have popcorn and watch our shows, Sundays we'd go to church at Greater House of Harmony, and it wasn't that bad. The temporary location was Moody's special events room, which made it convenient to stay for breakfast after. And we'd go and see Grandpa every day.

Someone began working on Unexpected House, the last two weeks of August. Winky and I tried to find out what was going on in there, but the yard, including the backyard where the secret fort is, was taped off with yellow crime scene tape and sawhorses. KEEP OUT, said the signs posted here and there. It was wicked maddening to have our space invaded like that. I've learned that I like to get answers to my questions, even if I don't end up liking the answer.

One afternoon, we were kicking the soccer ball around town. We kicked the ball all over the place, by the diner, and the post office, and Books 'n Things and the Pay 'n Takit. We walked by the construction site of what would be the Greater House of Harmony Church. We waved to Joe Viola. He was working with the Ladies' Auxiliary. The Ladies were all wielding hammers and slinging tool belts and showing Joe how to do everything.

When we went by Unexpected House, we were wicked surprised to see the crime scene tape was gone, and a man was stealing the FOR SALE sign from the front yard.

"I'm not stealing it," he said. "Why would I steal a FOR SALE sign? Somebody bought the place, I figure. Or the seller took it off the market. Or someone had a reversal of fortune." He looked up at the clouds and sighed a loud sigh. "I'm just the guy who puts up the signs and takes them down." He heaved the sign into the bed of his pickup truck.

We watched the sign guy drive off with the sign. We were signless.

"Now what?" said Winky.

"Nothing stopping us from going to the secret fort," I said. So we did that. I was worried that whoever had been messing around inside the house had messed around our fort. We hadn't been able to get back there for two whole weeks.

I parted the willow branches and we went into the fort.

Now there were *two* chairs, plus a lavender bath rug, with fringe. Winky made a Pope-like gesture to offer me the new chair, and he sat on the old chair. Then he opened up the fridge. By now we had grown used to seeing the Coleman cooler full of good stuff, and we'd even sort of started to take it for granted the snacks would magically appear and that none of it was poisoned. But this time, there was *more*. There was *cake*.

Winky took the cake out and inspected it with his magnifier. "Moody's coconut layer cake," he said. There were also two forks, real ones, not plastic, and so we dug right in. It felt like a party.

The silverware made me think of my plans to make money, the plans Winky'd said were one prong short of a typical fork. I didn't need to make money anymore, I guessed. But still. The final prong *was* going to be my dad. Child Protective Services reported there were no leads on finding a biological father. End of story. The coming so *close* to having one made the *not* having one seem more sad. It made me miss my mom.

Suddenly the cake didn't taste that great. Well, that's not true. It still tasted good, but I just couldn't eat any more.

"You okay?" said Winky.

"Yes," I said. "No. Yes and no." Either way, I'd lost my appetite.

"Knock-knock," came a voice.

Winky and I both jumped up. Carefully we drew aside the willow curtain, Winky on one side and me on the other.

"What are you doing here?" Winky asked Mrs. Blyth-Barrow, because it was *her* pretend-knocking at the sort-of door. "Not to be rude," he added.

"Josie. Winky," she said, looking at one of us and then the other, without a single flicker of surprise. "I own this house. Indeed I own *several* properties, and I recently realized I had reason to take this one off the market."

I thought about that. Mainly because it seemed like a tongue-twister.

"What reason did you recently realize?" Winky managed to ask after a second.

Mrs. Blyth-Barrow gave me a hard look. Not the hard look of Joe Viola staring down a batter. Not the hard look of Asa Pike ordering a rowdy Hot Dogs fan to simmer down. It was a look with lots of different pieces moving around in there like a kaleidoscope. I tried to make the pieces shift into a pattern.

"Was it you who kept stocking our fridge?" I asked.

Mrs. B-B's helmet hair didn't move an inch, but it was possible her eyes twinkled.

"Are you twinkling?" I said.

"Yes," she said, "I suppose I am twinkling a bit. I feel as though I might be."

"Are you taking this house off the market because you're going to live here? Is that why?" said Winky.

"Yes, indeed," said Mrs. Blyth-Barrow.

She smiled, and when she did, I saw she had one big gold tooth back in there. It was a nice tooth, an important tooth, like treasure stashed away for a rainy day.

"Josephine," she said, "I'm twinkling because I've been approved by Child Protective Services."

I didn't know what to say. "Oh," is all I came up with. What did it mean?

"Will you think about it?" said Mrs. B-B. "Would you like for this to be your home, too? With me?"

Oh! was all I could think. Then I thought about popcorn and TV night, the big stuffed chair, and the cats. I thought about the night the house burned down, how it was Mrs. B-B who hummed, and held me tight, and took me in.

"Well, you do play a pretty good game of soccer," I said.

"Of course I do," said Mrs. B-B. "In college, I captained . . . oh never mind about that," she said. "A story for another time."

"Okay," I said. My heart was fluttering and flapping like that feathered thing in Emily Dickinson's poem. That's right; I felt a surge of hope.

"Okay, what? Okay you want to live here," said Winky, "or okay, a story for another time?"

"Both," I said. Now I was happily floating on air, just like a lolling lily. (I don't know if that's accurate, because I never bothered to learn what a lolling lily is.) "I want to live here," I said, "and I want a story for another time. Both!"

There was some hugging, then, and a lot of smiling, and I found I could eat some more coconut layer cake after all.

Unexpected? You bet. It was wicked unexpected, right up till the very moment it happened.

"Well, *that* is . . . help me, now, what's the word I'm looking for . . ."Tina crossed her arms. "*Ugly*, is what." She shook her head. It was later that same day. We were already moving our things out of Kenerson's Five and Ten.

"It's unexpected!" I said.

"You got that right," Tina said. "You'd *expect* a house to have four walls and a roof. Where's the roof?"

"Actually, a geodesic dome makes a very solid structure," Joe said. He was totally on my team, about the house, and he'd picked up some engineering know-how from the Greater House of Harmony Ladies. "There isn't a right angle in the place, but it's solid, all right."

"You must see inside," I said. I knew all the selling points from two years of reading the for-sale flyers.

"It's larger than it looks," Winky said.

"It's a special opportunity," I reminded Tina.

"Well," Tina said. "A little paint. A little lovin'." She tilted her head to look from a different angle. "I suppose it *could* be charming."

The movers (Mr. Grigg, Debbie Moody-Cote,

Officer Pike, Joe Viola, and Mr. Mee) went to put
Mrs. B-B's stone angel in the yard. "No, no, that
goes *in*side, yes, inside!"

We had a housewarming party that very night,
and the whole town came. We had (more) cake,
and BBQ, and three different kinds of salad. When
it got dark, Mr. Mee dragged over some rocks to
make a fire ring, and then he built a campfire.
"I wasn't a Boy Scout for nothing," he said. And
who knew Rex Grigg could play the accordion?
Who knew Beverly Moody could sing? She tried
to teach us all an old French song. According to
Debbie Moody-Cote, it was a song mainly about
cabbages. It was pretty, just the same.

Winky was standing a little outside the fire
ring, outside the circle of people. On his magnifier,
firelight winked. I thought about Winky losing his
eyesight and with it the game he loved so much. I
thought about losing my mom, and Grandpa, too.
I think what I was most afraid of, all that time I
was scrambling to pay the mortgage and keep the
lights on, wasn't so much being without a house or
light to see by, but being without a family. I was
afraid I'd be alone: the great emergency of life. But
I wasn't alone.

I looked at all the people singing about

cabbages and roses, their faces glowing from the campfire and from all that togetherness. I wasn't alone at all.

What I remember most about that party is the stars in the sky, so clear and so many, beyond the dark curve of Unexpected House. Sometimes it happens that you look up from all that's been happening, and everything's changed. And you notice it's okay. You look up at the roof over your head, say, and maybe there isn't a right angle in the whole place, but it's a fine home, just the same. A wicked fine home, if you ask me.

Home

About One Year Later

Last Saturday, we all drove down to Boston for the annual Beep Ball Bash. Me and Tina went in the yellow Mustang with Grandpa and Mrs. B-B riding in the back seat. Mr. Mee drove down with the new teacher, Mr. DiAngelo, the one who replaced Mrs. B-B, in Mr. DiAngelo's Ford Pinto. Winky's parents took the bus. Winky, of course, was already there with his team: the Boston Bats.

"Peter Pan ain't so bad!" Mr. Wheaton said.

"No indeed, Bob," Mrs. Wheaton agreed. She'd been back and forth several times, ever since Brenda's Book Cozies had been picked up by a fancy shop in Boston called Noun: A Person's Place for Things. Mrs. Wheaton's good fortune was all thanks to orange lady, the one who had been so nice to us at the Beep Baseball Bash and explained to us the rules of the game. (Orange lady had a name, of course, and it was Michelle.) If you wonder how many people read books with covers they don't want anybody to see, the answer is: a lot.

"Sour ball?" Mr. Wheaton offered around a bag.

Mr. Mee sat beside me in a camp chair, with a book in his lap. There is a lot of waiting in baseball and in beep ball, and he said he likes to read during the lulls. Mr. DiAngelo sat on the other side of Mr. Mee and he drew in a sketchbook during the lulls. Lulls happen when Coach Viola stops the play to give a pep talk to the batter, for example.

Yes, *that* was my brilliant idea! Joe Viola needed a job, and the Beep Baseball League needed a coach! Coaching is a volunteer position, but Development Director is not. That's the person who brings in the money. Donations to the not-for-profit BBL are up, way up. Winky was right about his sports hero being a money-making *machine*.

It was the bottom of the ninth, and pitcher–coach–Development Director Joe was on the pitcher's mound doing such a wild wind-up for the crowd, his wide-striped shirt was coming untucked.

"Love ya, Joey!" Tina shouted. She can really belt it. "Tuck your shirt in!"

I leaned over to Mr. Mee. "Isn't this wicked?" I said.

Mr. Mee glanced up from his book.

"I mean, you know . . . everything?" I said.

"Indeed," said Mr. Mee. He poked the nose of his glasses. He seemed like he was waiting for me to say something else.

"Here we all are," I said, "when a year ago . . . basically a year ago *today* . . . my house burned down, and I thought it was the end of the world." I looked around at everybody from town who'd come to see the game. Mrs. Moody even brought *beignets*. "Wicked."

Mr. Mee took off his glasses and breathed on each lens. "Unlikely coincidences and stunning reversals are quite common in literature," he said. He wiped the glasses on the tail of his shirt. "If you had read more novels, you'd be better prepared for the seeming whimsy of this world and all of human existence."

I thought about that.

"Or," I said, "I could read *Ripley's Believe It or Not! Long Stories Edition*."

Mr. Mee put his glasses back on and went back to his book, but I saw a smile at the corner of his mouth. "Try a little Shakespeare," he said.

Winky stepped up to the plate.

We all went quiet as a golf match.

Joe lined it up—"Ready!"—and—"ball!"—let it fly.

Beep beep beep (the ball and) *Thock!* (the bat and) "Two!" (the spotter and) *Bzzzzzztzzzzzz* (the base and)—

Winky threw down the bat and started to run.

"Put one on the board, baby!" yelled Mrs. B-B.

Grandpa leaped to his feet like a man half his age. "Bananas! Baked beans!"

Mr. Mee and Mr. DiAngelo dropped their stuff on the ground and started going nuts!

Winky had thirty seconds to reach that base. I was clapping so hard my hands were stinging.

The ball went right by the first fielder.

"Run, Winky!"

It bounced toward the second fielder.

"Winky, go!"

That guy went to scoop up the ball, but it took a bad hop and bobbled out of his glove.

"Run, Winky!"

Another fielder crouched low to get the ball while the spotters kept yelling directions.

"*Dépêchez-vous!*" cried Mrs. Moody. Nobody knew what it meant, but we got the idea!

"Run it in, Elwyn, sweetie, you can do it!" yelled Mrs. Wheaton, flapping her arms like a big flowery bird.

I don't know if the pitcher was supposed to be screaming, but there was Joe Viola hollering, "Go go go go go!"

We were all of us on our feet, yelling and screaming and jumping up and down and I must have been yelling loudest of all: "Go Winkeeeeee!"

And guess what—do you believe it?

I bet you do.

Winky ran it home.